DANGEROUS ALIBIS

AF877142

by

Carolyn Chambers Clark, Ed.D., R.N.

Vista publishing, Inc.

COPYRIGHT © 1994 by Carolyn Chambers Clark

All rights reserved. No part of this book may be reproduced or transmitted in any form or by any means, graphic, electronic, or mechanical, including photocopying, recording, or any information storage or retrieval system, for sale, without written permission from the author, except for brief quotations included in a review.

Edited by Mary Ann Liotta, RN

Cover Art Work by Noelle Auriemma
Graphic Production by Thomas Taylor of Thomcatt Graphics

Vista Publishing, Inc.
473 Broadway
Long Branch, NJ 07740
(908) 229-6500

This publication is designed for the reading pleasure of the general public. All characters, places, situations, and events are fictional and are in no way intended to depict actual people or situations.

First Edition

ISBN: 1-880254-16-6
Library of Congress Catalog Card Number: 94-60517

U.S.A. Price: $9.95
Canada Price: $15.95

DEDICATION

This book is dedicated to three wonderful friends and colleagues

Susan Farese
Sandi Epstein
Sandy Oestreich

Thanks a bunch for your support, networking contacts, and cheery dispositions.

SPECIAL THANKS

I appreciate the invaluable assistance of the following: Anthony Auriemma; Chip Wood; Alice Morrow, Administrative Assistant and Volunteer Coordinator, and Officer Johnson, Public Information Officer for the St. Petersburg Police Department; Tim Moran, Medical Examiner's Office, Pinellas County; Kate Richards, Private Investigator; and, the Don CeSar Beach Resort for allowing me to use a photo of their beautiful hotel on the cover of Dangerous Alibis.

MEET THE AUTHOR

Carolyn Chambers Clark, Ed.D., R.N.

Carolyn Chambers Clark earned a B.S. in Nursing from the University of Wisconsin-Madison, a Masters Degree in Psychiatric/Mental Health Nursing from Rutgers, the State University, New Jersey, and a doctorate in Nursing Education from Teachers College, Columbia University, New York City. She is an Advanced Registered Nurse Practitioner (ARNP) in Psychiatric/Mental Health Nursing and was admitted as a Fellow to the American Academy of Nursing in 1980.

She is the Editor of *ALTERNATIVE HEALTH PRACTITIONER: THE JOURNAL OF COMPLEMENTARY AND NATURAL CARE* and is listed in WHO'S WHO OF AMERICAN WOMEN.

Carolyn's work experiences are extensive and varied. She has thirty years of experience as a clinician, educator, consultant and psychotherapist. She has taught thousands of nurses at the baccalaureate, graduate and continuing education level. She has published nine textbooks and numerous book chapters, continuing education programs, learning systems and articles.

In 1980, Carolyn founded THE WELLNESS INSTITUTE, offering wellness workshops, consultation and a health promotion newsletter. Since 1980, she has been the editor/publisher of *THE WELLNESS NEWSLETTER*, which she developed to fill the void of self-care information.

Currently she provides continuing education self-study courses and workshops for nurses in Florida; maintains a private practice in individual, couple and family psychotherapy and therapeutic touch; teaches self-esteem, stress management and self-awareness courses for the community; and, provides therapeutic touch workshops for nurses and others interested in learning the skill.

Carolyn has lived in Florida with her husband, Tony, since 1984. One of his daughters, Noelle, created the hotel drawings for the book cover. Carolyn enjoys early morning walks on the beach, tap dancing and puttering with her plants.

CHAPTER ONE

When Ted Sampson first walked into my office, I could have sworn he wanted me to tail his wife. Boy, was I wrong.

I'd been out most of the morning taking pictures of a guy who was injured at work and was suing the city of St. Petersburg for big bucks. When I arrived back at my Central Avenue office, Sampson was standing outside my door, waiting patiently. The elevator was on the blink again, so when I came up the stairs, huffing more than I'd like, I saw him. He was reading the black painted letters of my name and business scrawled across the bubbled glass of my door:

Theresa Franco
Private Investigator

His expression was warm, friendly. "Are you Ms. Franco?" he said. Great voice.

I nodded and gave him what I hoped was a brilliant smile. I don't have a reception area or a secretary and the hall is my waiting room. But since Earl, the cleaning man, was waxing the floor, and my ficus plants were closing in on us, Ted Sampson had barely enough standing room in the corridor. Even with that, he looked at ease, as if he faced similar obstacles every day. He was tall and thin, maybe ten years ahead of me, but on him it looked good. I'd never met the guy before, but there was something familiar about him. Maybe it was his gorgeous blue eyes, so deep they seemed to go on forever, or it might have been his muscular body that gave me that déjà vu feeling. It might have even been the way the light played across his wavy graying hair. So sexy.

Then it hit me. The guy was a Paul Newman lookalike.

Women tend to hate me at first because they think my life is all glamor and excitement. They come to my office expecting to find a gun-toting, loud-mouthed, Hollywood fantasy type like the ones on TV. Of course once they get to know me, they find out I'm a forty-year-old grandmother who's a private investigator, one of the 3,807 members of the Florida Association of Licensed Investigators.

Men see me a little differently. I wondered what he thought of my five-foot-four frame with its 130 pounds fairly well-packed into Bill Blass size 10 cotton pants. My rayon blouse was the perfect shade to bring out the green in my hazel eyes, the cosmetic consultant at Loehmann's had told me. I didn't have time to check his reaction because as my taupe flats navigated around Arnold's water pail, I slid across the waxed surface nearly into Ted Sampson's arms. He quickly stepped forward, grabbed my elbow and brought me in for a two-point landing. I murmured my appreciation and pretended I wasn't flustered.

I prefer brains over brawn everytime and he looked like the intellectual type to me, but I have been known to be wrong. I'm not that strong myself, and my only concession to getting more powerful is a daily struggle with two-pound weights, but that's only to keep my underarms from getting flabby. After thirty-five, you have to do that, whether you're an investigator or not.

I forced myself to behave, although standing that close to an attractive man usually brings out the zany in me. He was very polite, holding my camera for me while I opened the door. Then he stood calmly in the tiny entryway that's no bigger than an elevator car, until I motioned him to a straight-backed chair opposite mine at the desk.

My office is not exactly a set for a tough guy detective story. It abuts the Tampa Bay Insurance Agency, my ex-husband's company. I used to work with him, but our connections, both personal and professional have loosened considerably lately. Some people, including my kids, say it's stupid for me to work so close to him, but it was part of the settlement to get use of the office in exchange for an occasional insurance-related job for him. With rents the way they are and the competition in the field, I couldn't turn it down.

My office feels cozy and comfortable because I made it that way. Macrame hangings and needlepointed footrests make me feel right at home. Since the divorce, most of the time, it is my home. Sometimes I fall asleep there, so I don't want to wake up with a cricked neck. My Lazy-Boy may not be high fashion, but it's fine for a catnap or hours of report writing. Opposite that is the bookcase I bought at a garage sale. It's crammed with books on disguise, Florida law, and all my texts from Career City College. I can't bear to give things away, even when they've worn out their usefulness.

The old mahogany desk I found in a second hand store and refinished. I like it because it reminds me of my father, a retired police captain who collects antiques. The desk sits by my only window, overlooking Central Avenue. Ted Sampson leaned forward and said, "I'm sorry to just drop by without an appointment, but I am in a big hurry."

"No problem," I said, feeling a second chill of recognition.

"A mutual friend recommended you." He passed me my card and I passed it back.

I stared at his sun-tanned face. "And who might that be?" I had a few friends around town and I wondered who had been kind enough to send me this hunk.

"Aaron Feinstein."

Mr. Feinstein was a slick lawyer who was accused of his wife's murder a couple of years ago, but got off with a good alibi. The police pinned the whole thing on a thief who had been in the Feinstein house robbing them about the time

Mrs. Feinstein died. I didn't trust Aaron Feinstein and I had no idea why he would refer anyone to me.

Ted Sampson had no visible mannerisms and looked as cool and calm as a well-trained actor, but when he studied me carefully, I felt my face start to heat up. I was probably red as a school girl contemplating the object of her first crush. But then, I do tend to blush rather easily. Being careful to gauge my words, I said, "I know Mr. Feinstein, but I doubt if he's a friend."

He smiled. A fabulous smile with just the right balance between seduction and respect. "He speaks highly of you."

Always a sucker for flattery, I smiled and relaxed back into my chair. I thought, why not enjoy this? Even if he wants me to follow up on his abducted kid, or make sure he gets all his money from his insurance company, being in his presence ought to more than make up for the tedious task ahead.

Then he surprised me.

"What's that?" he said, pointing to my fax machine.

I smiled, thinking he was probably teasing. "It's my fax. Another wonder of the electronic age that enables me to have just enough repair bills to offset my income." He smiled back and I nearly forgot where the conversation was going.

The fish tank in the corner was gurgling softly, but it sounded like Rachmaninoff to me. "Coffee?" I said, hoping to delay the more uninteresting part of my job.

"No, thanks. Never drink the stuff. Find it makes me hyper."

I glanced at him again and saw his face had gone taut. I wouldn't exactly call it malice, but it was something quite close. For a second, it scared me. Then I noticed he was wearing a rather out-of-date suit and that endeared him to me again. My dad has never been known for his fancy dress and at that moment something in Ted Sampson's face reminded me of dear old dad. He couldn't be too bad a person if he reminded me of my father, so I pulled out two V-8 juices from a small refrigerator next to my desk and offered him one.

He declined that, too. I was running out of things to offer him. I snapped off the aluminum lid on mine and took a deep swallow, then put the can in front of me. Without skipping a beat, I turned back to my notebook in which I was writing important information, including his height, weight, the exact blue of his eyes, and the broadness of his shoulders.

He interrupted my concentrated action with his words. "I suppose you want to know what I'm doing here."

I sat back in my chair again and made full eye contact with the guy. I realized then I didn't care one way or the other if he hired me as long as he stuck around. Knowing full well I was being corny beyond words, I murmured, "And why's that?"

"I want to hire you to find something for me."

I glanced at his ring finger. No ring. Either he was married and didn't wear one or he wasn't married. I was hoping for the latter. I took a long sip on my V-8, then asked, "Just what do you need to find?"

"It's a diary."

"Yours?"

I had thought his eyes were indigo at first, but now I saw they were more a lavender blue. His glance was level, serious, as though some inner light needed tending. For all his good looks, he seemed to be a guy who needed an infusion of love. I somehow sensed there was more to his story than he was telling.

Maybe it was only my wish that he had come to me for more. After all, I'd been pretty lonely after my divorce. A double date with my son and his wife and a car salesman did not a romantic evening make.

He hesitated, then said, "The diary belonged to Aaron Feinstein."

"Your friend and mine."

"Actually, he's not my friend at all. He's the reason I've been off the streets for a while, don't know what a fax machine is, and haven't had a good night's sleep in four years."

I smiled at him. My clients often lie to me at first. Either they think they have to protect someone or they aren't sure they can trust me. Once they start leveling, I am more inclined to work with them. Now I knew why the guy looked familiar. I'd seen his picture four years ago in the trial for Mrs. Feinstein's murder. Ted Sampson was the one who went to prison for her death.

He had none of the look of prison about him, but then he was probably the kind of guy who exercised religiously, cell or no cell. He may even have watched what he ate. Especially if he was vain enough.

"When were you released?"

"Yesterday."

"How's it feel?"

He smiled. "Great. Better than I thought. I've been eating non-stop since I got out. I'll tell you lobster and hamburgers can taste pretty good."

He gave me a boyish smile and that was when I really started believing him. When I saw his picture in the paper during the trial years ago, I remembered thinking: this is not the face of a murderer. I probably already knew the answer to my next question, but I asked it anyway. "Just why do you want the diary?"

His eyes lit up, this time a deeper blue. Prussian, I think. The emotion in his voice convinced me. "That diary is going to prove he killed his wife, that's why."

With adrenalin pumping through my little fingers, I started to write on another sheet of paper. This was going to be the case that made me famous, the case that broke me out of taking photos of cracked sidewalks and dressing like a bag lady. I looked up at Ted Sampson and said in the steadiest voice I could summon, "You want to fill me in on this?"

"Sure." He leaned back in his chair, looking totally relaxed. "Feinstein invited me to his house the night his wife was murdered. Only he neglected to tell me he was planning to kill her."

"A set-up?"

"You got it."

"Why would he want to frame you?"

"I was just stupid. He was looking for a scapegoat and he sure found one in me."

"How did he get you over to his house late at night?"

"If you know Feinstein, you know he does most of his business at night. He had been after me for weeks to invest in a printing company he owns. He'd made it sound like such a good deal, I'd been interested, but just couldn't find the time to discuss it. He suggested a meeting at his house. He even told me that if I arrived first, to ring the bell and his wife would let me in."

"What happened when you got there?"

"The front door was half-open and I had a definite feeling something was wrong. I suppose I should have turned and left, but knowing his wife was there made me think maybe I should see if she was all right."

"She was dead."

"Yes. Kind of makes you want to turn your back on helping people, you know?"

"I know."

"Especially when I had all those free hours in my cell to figure out what the frame-up was about."

"What did you figure?"

He leaned over my desk and cocked an eyebrow. "I haven't got all the pieces, but I think he was connected, if you know what I mean."

I knew what he meant. There had been rumors circulating around St. Petersburg that more than a few people were deep into organized crime or at least into huge drug deals. Although I never suspected Feinstein, thinking about it, he was just the type to be involved. So far, Ted Sampson's story sounded plausible, but I needed more information. I looked back at him. "Just what is in the diary?"

"Feinstein is a meticulous man. He keeps track of every time he goes to the bathroom. He has to have made notes about setting me up. There should be names, places, dates and everything I need to get my credibility back."

"Okay, sounds like a good place to start."

"Then you'll take me on as a client?"

"Tentatively. I need to check a few things first. I'll call you later." He looked disappointed. Gray had entered those beautiful blue eyes and I almost recanted then and there. Courage I told myself. Let him wait a few hours. The trail isn't going to get any colder than it is now. I also didn't want to upset good investigative procedure and I was afraid that if I didn't get away from him for a little while I might just do something really stupid.

He stood up and handed me a card. "You can reach me here. Anytime." I admired a guy who could get a business card printed in a day. I almost asked him how he had achieved such a wondrous feat, but thought better of it. I stood up and we shook hands. His grip was warm, firm and sent a shock wave through me. Talk about your chemical reactions.

He let go of my hand before I was ready. He nodded and said, "Don't forget to call."

"I won't," I said.

* * *

I had a few delightful tasks to handle first. Like taking pictures of the site of a fire on the corner of First Avenue South and Highway 19. The insurance company suspected arson, but I thought they were probably whistling in the dark on that. I've been at this business for eight years now, having graduated with honors from Career City College in Fort Lauderdale. I got interested in investigative work when someone broke into our home and the police couldn't come up with a single suspect. Most of what I do is dressing for success, not tracking down vicious killers. One day I had to don the garb of a bag lady and dig through someone's trash to get information. Dirty business. Another time I had a facial, coifed my raven locks, pulled on a tight fringed dress to accentuate my curves and put on four-inch heels. Then I came on to my client's husband to see if he was fooling around. That one was fun.

Other times, I dress like a housewife and turn on the charm. When I mention I'm the grandmother of a two-year-old to a distressed parent, I'm halfway home. Who's not going to talk to a grandma?

Murder is rare, if not nonexistent, in my line of work. Some of what I do is darn right tedious work. Once I had to track down a defense witness in a death penalty case. Starting with previous addresses, I traced the suspect to northern Pinellas County. The whole business took several days, many phone calls and a lot of leg work. What I do doesn't fit nicely into a 50-minute television show format, but it pays the bills.

Some of the most useful things I know I learned in acting class. Being a private investigator is drama of the highest order. I've posed as a janitor in a warehouse, a cashier in a hardware store and a waitress in a restaurant in employee theft cases. Private investigators are primarily information gatherers. Most of my cases involve fraud, insurance-related investigations, accidents, personal injury cases, abducted kids, cheating spouses, or missing assets.

The worst part of the job is the discrimination I face. Even though my teachers always said woman are better detail people and generally better communicators than men, nine times out of ten when the phone rings in my office, the caller asks to speak with the boss man. When I worked at the Dale Agency, there were a couple of male investigators who called me sweet pea and sweetie. That used to really irk me, until I found out women have to deal with that kind of putdown wherever they work.

But I wouldn't give up being a woman for anything. One of the greatest advantages of what I do is my low profile. Being female comes in mighty handy when doing surveillance work. Nobody suspects a dippy-looking female. Especially not macho males. They're also the least likely to expect a woman to follow them. Even if they catch on to being tailed, they're extremely flattered.

One of the disadvantages of my job is the hours. I work everyday, weekends and nights. That is what brought about the demise of my marriage. That and the fact Mike couldn't keep away from his secretary. The hours I work do make for flexibility and luckily I don't need much sleep, because sometimes I work straight through the day and night.

Danger? Sure, there's some of that. I do have to be more cautious when I work in rough parts of town. I carry a stun gun and tear gas but I've never had to use either. Like I said, brains over brawn.

I left my office shortly after Ted Sampson did. I really wanted to leave with him and see what kind of car he drove, what he looked like in the sunshine, how it felt to walk next to him and other important investigative details, but I forced myself to wait five minutes by the clock in my office before leaving.

My Toyota made a few sputters when I pulled out of the parking lot, telling me it was overdue for a tune-up. In this business, you don't have time for things like visits to the service station. I usually end up waiting until it breaks down and then renting a car in the interim.

I swung onto Central, hearing the cartons of clothes and other aspects of my traveling disguise show banging around behind me. Since I'm not always sure what I'll need when I'm working on a case, I carry most of my quick-change wardrobe with me, along with client files, a few reference books, notepaper, a jug of filtered water, some high-protein snacks, a couple of raunchy novels and an extra pillow. Everything I need to fill those long hours of surveillance work.

I thought about Ted as I drove. He probably couldn't be entirely trusted. None of my clients could, but then again, would anyone with a face like that tell more than a few white lies? I doubted it.

I tried to remember what I knew about Aaron Feinstein. He was a corporate lawyer who had a reputation for taking on environmental polluters as his clients. Aaron was outwardly gracious and warm. Peel that surface layer away and underneath was a cold, unscrupulous man who would do anything for money. He kept to himself after hours, but could be involved in even dirtier deals outside court, if Ted Sampson was to be believed.

I had found Aaron a gentleman with no sense of humor and a lousy memory. Maybe he did keep a diary to remind himself of important happenings. It made sense.

But could whatever was in that diary prove Ted Sampson hadn't killed Feinstein's wife? I had no idea. As I recall, Mrs. Feinstein had a lover, Dell Channing. His name came up at the trial, but then disappeared. That would be something to check into.

If what Ted Sampson said was true, Feinstein had to have a motive for killing his wife. I wondered what it was. Dell Channing's name kept buzzing around in my brain. Maybe Feinstein was jealous of the way his wife flaunted her affair. Maybe he thought killing her would be the way to get back at Dell. Stranger things have happened.

I tried to remember the details of the trial. Aaron Feinstein had been meeting with a client in Tampa the night his wife had been murdered. Convenient. He didn't arrive home until after the police got there. Mrs. Feinstein was bludgeoned with a brass dolphin from the mantle in the living room. The weapon was found beside her, wiped clean of fingerprints by a linen napkin, also found on the floor. Tables had been overturned, curtains slashed and drawers ransacked. The police had concluded she had caught Ted Sampson in the act of trying to recover some incriminating evidence and had been murdered.

The DA managed to convince the jury that Ted Sampson had motive and he certainly had access. The DA argued Ted was involved in a questionable business deal and Aaron Feinstein was about to blow the whistle on him. Witnesses were produced to substantiate Feinstein's claim and the jury believed him, Paul Newman's looks notwithstanding. He was handsome, he was caught with the dead woman. Citizens were curious, headlines blistered across the front page of the ***Times***. Too juicy for words.

CHAPTER TWO

St. Petersburg is a Central Florida town of nearly 250,000, a sleepy big city that is small town America. It sits majestically between Tampa Bay and the sparkling Gulf of Mexico and used to be known as the retirement capital of the world, but in past years, the average age of residents has moved rapidly downward. St. Petersburg is really a cluster of towns. Most are well-cared for, many have ethnic orientations. Some are in transition. Palm trees and oleanders are everywhere, as are shocking purple jacaranda, pigeon plums, bottle brush, and orchid trees.

High-rise modern, glass and stone bank buildings stand on Central Avenue interspersed with one and two-story stucco office buildings of a decidedly Mediterranian style. The police department is located downtown between Central Avenue and First Avenue North on the busy one-way street known as Thirteenth. It takes up two buildings, the older one concrete with a marble interior, the newer, more ugly one, mostly concrete and steel.

Winter in St. Petersburg lasts about two weeks in January when the temperature dips into the thirties. The rainy season, which is also the hurricane season, lasts well into the fall, but the greatest rain comes in the summer before Labor Day. Six months of the year the temperature is in the humid nineties. This was September and it was hot.

I went into the Homicide Department to see Lieutenant Jefferson. Steve is in his early fifties and has the look of a sergeant in the Marine Corps: nearly gray crewcut, bushy eyebrows, piercing brown eyes that give you the once over and size you up in a second, a crooked nose that looks as if it has been broken a few times, round face, and creased forehead. His body is big, but firm, his hands, huge. His dark, hawkish face looks at times as if it has never known a smile, but when he saw me, he smiled, a broad, boyish grin.

Steve is a smart man. He's caught more than his quota of thieves and killers. Once in a while he guesses wrong and sometimes he's tempted to look the other way when someone he likes steps over the letter of the law, and to be merciless when someone he doesn't even breathes heavy.

He'd probably already figured out what I was doing there. Steve knew the sight of me meant I was sniffing around for information. He most likely hadn't narrowed down the case, but then again, he might have had a good idea if he knew Ted Sampson had just been released from prison.

Steve is a friend of my father's and so allows me a little more slack than he does the average investigator. I take advantage of his kindnesses whenever I can.

When I was younger, I refused to let people help me. Now that I'm older and a little grayer, I welcome it just as long as it's deserved. I usually manage to talk myself into thinking it is.

He motioned me back to his office, patting my shoulder, just like my dad would do. His office is small, tiny. He didn't close the door behind us. I think he tries to keep up with whatever is happening around him and feels left out if he misses even the slightest incident. Or maybe he was just checking up on his detectives. He is responsible for them getting their reports in on time and bringing in suspects for questioning and he rides them like a herd.

"What can I do you for?" he said, but his tone was tired, weary. I suspected he'd had a rough day already and probably didn't need an investigator poking around his shop.

"I want to look up the files on Ted Sampson."

He gave me a grudging nod. "Um hm. You know it's against department policy

I put on my most demure look. "Come on, Steve. Help me out on this, will you?"

"Jeez." He gazed out into the hall as if the solution to his dilemma might reside there. "If it were any other---"

"You've given me information before."

He shook his head firmly. "The case is closed."

"Then what's the big deal?"

He inspected me as if I was on the auction block. "The guy killed Mrs. Feinstein and it was proved in a court of law. He's done his time and that's that."

"He wants to vindicate himself."

"I know. He's already been here, trying to look at the files himself."

"He has?" That floored me. It was not only strange, it wasn't very smart. What could Ted Sampson possibly learn from the files he didn't already know? He'd been questioned and must have heard all the other evidence the police had at the trial.

"Isn't that somethin'? I think your client has a screw loose."

"He's not my client yet."

"Maybe you'd better rethink taking this guy on." He shook his head, this time slowly, looking at me as if I might be more than a little gullible. "This one's a real pip."

"Yeah, isn't he. I don't know yet if I'm taking the case." That was a lie. I'd already decided I would, but I wasn't going to let Steve know that. I tried out my professional smile. "Just want to check some details."

"At least you haven't lost everything your father taught you."

How he knew what my father taught me, I wasn't sure, but I guess he had visions of what a good policeman teaches his daughter. Since Steve was single and had never married or fathered any children that I knew of, his visions were probably mostly technicolor dreams, the kind Walt Disney puts on the screen.

We waited in silence, he staring at me, me staring right back. Finally I said, "So what's it going to be?"

A slight smile started on the edge of his lips and travelled across his face. "Jeez, Theresa, you're as hard-nosed as that hothead father of yours."

"Could be. Now, what about the files?"

"I'd give them to you, but there may be something still operating in this one."

My heart skipped a beat. "Like what?"

"You know I can't tell you that."

"Then give me a hint."

He crossed his arms in front of his chest and consulted the ceiling. I looked up and saw a spider high-tailing it across the speckled surface. After a minute he said, "No hints, but I'll let you see the old file. Only on one condition. " I crossed my heart and raised my hand for the oath. "Very funny. I better not hear any complaints about how you're browbeating witnesses or harrassing my men---" I shook my head and he grimaced, then picked up the phone and asked Records to send up the files. When he hung up, he sucked on his teeth for a moment, looking at me with a mixture of frustration and admiration. "You are some case, Theresa, some case."

"I know. Just like my father." We both smiled, knowing we had achieved an uneasy truce. Then I sat politely listening to him tell me about my dad and the good old times until the files arrived.

"You can use my office," he said, "I've got to go out anyway." I wasn't sure whether he was leaving to oblige me or whether he really did have an appointment. Whichever, I sat down at his desk as soon as he left and started sorting through the papers.

It was all pretty much as Ted had reported. He'd been found in the Feinstein house by the police, questioned and sounded guilty as hell. Dell Channing had been questioned extensively, then let go. I flipped through copies of reports, trying to piece together all the facts. I made notes, jotting down last-known addresses and telephone numbers which were probably out of date, but if I let Ted Sampson hire me, as I knew I would, they might spark further information.

My fingers stopped on a series of faxed memos from the Tallahassee Police Department about a second homicide. At first I thought it was a case of mistaken filing, then I saw Roberto Ramon, owner of Greener Grass, had been a regular employee of Aaron Feinstein. Why would Feinstein murder someone who cut his grass? Weirder and weirder.

I paged through a number of terse memorandums and penciled summations of telephone calls. Two detectives had even been sent to Tallahassee to discuss the case. After their visit, messages continued to fly back and forth between the St. Petersburg and Tallahassee police departments for days. One memo noted that a key to Aaron Feinstein's back door had been found in Roberto Ramon's bedroom.

Had Roberto and Mrs. Feinstein been playing footsie or was he given a key to the house for other reasons? A lengthy interview with Roberto Ramon's mother hadn't added any important details. Roberto's widow had been something else. She had seemed convinced that someone had been trailing Roberto and even threatened his life. The description fit Ted Sampson. When Roberto was nearly run over by a truck, he left and ran for cover to Tallahassee, where he had friends. Two days later he was dead, bludgeoned with a heavy object.

Same method. It was the kind of murder either a man or woman could pull off. Even a small woman could come from behind and bring a brick or statue crashing down. The other person wouldn't have a chance, no matter if he was a muscular yard worker or the wife of a powerful lawyer.

No summary statement tied any of the interviews or memos together. The connection between Aaron Feinstein's alleged murderer and Roberto Ramon's appeared to be Ted Sampson. Except there was no proof.

My mind was already spinning, trying to think of what woman might have a motive and access to murder both people. Just before I closed up the file, a penciled summation of a telephone call from an anonymous source caught my eye. Someone with a female voice had called the police at 8:45 P.M. and reported a disturbance at 765 Dewberry Lane, the Feinstein residence, just about the time Ted told the police he was walking in the front door of Aaron Feinstein's house. It could have been a neighbor who'd heard the commotion when Mrs. Feinstein had been killed. If it had been, there was no mention of that person ever coming forward. The woman could also have been Feinstein's accomplice, meaning that Ted Sampson was right, he was set up.

I rubbed my hands together in excitement. I could hardly wait to get started talking to people. In the back of my mind I was already being interviewed on Channel 8, telling them how I cleared Ted Sampson of an unjust confinement in Raiford State Prison.

Lieutenant Jefferson came back to claim his office just as I was getting ready to leave. I was glad to see him because I had a few questions to ask him. He gave me another of his boyish grins. "I told you there might be something still operating."

"You think Ted Sampson killed both Mrs. Feinstein and Roberto Ramon?"

"You bet."

"Then why wasn't this brought out in the trial?"

"We couldn't make it stick."

"And you still can't, can you? Everything is circumstantial evidence."

"That's right."

I stared out the small window to my left, noticing how the window cleaners missed a spot just east of center. I didn't like the implication that my soon-to-be-signed client might be guilty of two murders.

The lieutenant tightened his face and a little vein in his forehead started to pulsate. "I could have nailed him real good but Harpen, that damned D.A. with the big mouth and the small brain, was in a hurry. She didn't want her case jeopardized. It smelled to high heaven of city politics."

I looked away, this time at the mug of cold coffee on the windowsill. "So how come you let me see all that?"

He shrugged. "Maybe I want to see what you can do."

"You think I can do more than the St. Petersburg and Tallahassee police departments?" Even I didn't think I was that good.

"I don't know. I know we worked on connecting the two for months. So did Tallahassee. We didn't turn up much. No fingerprints on that one either. We couldn't place Sampson at the scene in Tallahasse and couldn't find any witnesses."

"That's why you let me see the files?"

He nodded and sat down on the edge of the desk. "I think you're a pretty good investigator. That fiasco with Fletcher and Hingroove last year proved that. I figure you might turn up something we couldn't."

Just by the way he said it, made me think someone had been stepping on a few toes and closing a few political doors for the local police. I didn't know if Aaron Feinstein had that kind of clout or not, but I was about to find out.

It was nearly 5:00 when I got back to my office. I got another V-8 out of my refrigerator and threw back the whole thing in one gulp. Sometimes I live dangerously. I went out into the small garden behind the building Mike had paid a nursery to concoct. A couple of banana trees stood next to an avocado and tangelo tree. Mike's idea of a garden was not flowers. He wanted it to produce edible fruit. He was always more practical than I.

Sitting on the stone ledge, I inhaled the basil and peppermint plants and thought about Ted Sampson. I had already decided to accept him as a client, even if he did have strange tendencies. Shortly after that I called in to my answering service and left.

* * *

The place I call home, even if I'm hardly ever there, is on the beach. I rent one-half of a one-story pink stucco with a red tile roof. It looks exactly like the others on the block except for the color. I have to walk eight blocks to the beach, but when the wind is right, I can smell the salt air as strong as if I lived on the Gulf.

Most of the homes around me are owned by retirees or rented by snowbirds who come for the season, usually October to April. My landlady, Evelyn Rosecki, is a widow, a retired ballerina who now makes her living by composing greeting cards. She likes to try them out on me. Most are too saccharine, but she sells them. Lord only knows how. She tells me she saves money by taking her dinners out, dining between 4:00 and 6:00 P.M. when the earlybird specials are in force. She has to fight off the hordes of like-minded senior citizens, but she thinks it's worth it. She only shops at stores that give double coupons and claims she gets food for most of her other meals on less than $10.00 a week.

If I had heroes, which I don't anymore, Evelyn would qualify. She's a feisty lady with a lot of grit. We have an ongoing argument about whether private investigation is a suitable profession for a lady, but otherwise I'd vote her in for anybody's mom, including mine, if I had the chance.

My portion of the house has a separate entrance and pretty good insulation. The only time I hear noises from her side of the house is when Sheba, her cat, brings home a dead bird and Evelyn bawls her out or when she puts on her Frank Sinatra records and turns up the volume. I have managed to make the one-bedroom abode comfortable by strategic placement of ficus trees in straw pots, white wicker furniture, peach cushions and needlepointed pillows, fluffy white throw rugs across the terrazzo floor, peach curtains at the bay windows and my daughter's oil paintings of flowers and fruits on the off-white walls. My bedroom is just big enough for a rattan settee, single bed, small desk, bookshelf and hand weights.

I installed ceiling fans in every room because I hate air conditioning. I try to get along without it between September and May and sometimes I manage it.

The kitchen and bath need new fixtures and cabinets, but I made the rooms livable with a little paint and plants that can make it on their own for up to a week. I'm away for extended periods of time on surveillance. Comes with the territory.

CHAPTER THREE

I hate spending evenings alone, so I often hang out on the beach at the Tiki Bar. It looks out over the Gulf of Mexico on Redington Beach and there's always a breeze there, even when the temperature is 90 degrees. It's the sort of place where you can stand under a palm tree, lounge on the beach, or even sit at one of the white metal tables and sip a soda without a waitress bothering you. They also serve sandwiches, salads and some pretty good fish and chicken dishes. There is always music, usually an unknown singer hoping to be discovered, who plays a guitar and sings ballads.

Customers dance near the bandstand. I've even seen a couple, locked in a passionate embrace, waltz on the sand in the moonlight. The bar is very close to the water, standing next to the swimming pool of the hotel it belongs to. I never go in the hotel, it's too full of tourists, but the outside tables and beach are populated by quite a few locals who, like me, love the water, the music, the breeze and occasional conversation.

The tourists tend to cluster around the pool, or under the thatched roof of the bar, ordering drinks from their lounge chairs or diving into the water and shouting to each other. We tolerate them and they don't bother us too much. The place appeals to me because I don't have to dress up, worry about my make-up or pay attention to anyone. If I want, I can just sink into a lounge chair behind an oleander and not even be seen. Benjie's cooking is imaginative, sort of Floridian with a Cajun twist. Benjie and Evelyn are pretty good friends and sometimes I wonder if romance is not in the offing, but Evelyn denies such frivolousness.

Benjie is in his sixties, younger than Evelyn, but the two of them get along quite well, except for occasional bickering. I don't even know his last name. Everyone uses just Benjie. He is a native Floridian, one of the few. He loves to go fishing on his time off and sometimes takes Evelyn with him. He has a walnut complexion and a shiny, bald head. His body is well-muscled and he has a shaggy mustache that he sometimes rearranges with his fingers when he talks. He wears Hawaiian shirts of explosive colors, white shorts and sneakers.

That night when Ted Sampson walked to the small bar, he hesitated, surveying the tables. When he located me, he moved past the gawkers who weren't quite sure if they recognized him or not. He was wearing white slacks and a red shirt. Fabulous. I wished I'd put on my green silk dress and at least combed my hair. My Bill Blass pants sported a dab of dried V-8 juice and my rayon blouse clung uncomfortably to my back. Ted Sampson looked freshly showered and smelled like a pine forest when he slipped into a chair opposite me at the table and flashed me a smile.

Benjie misses nothing and he is a very protective guy who is convinced I am in an unhealthy line of business. He ambled over, eyeing Ted uneasily, probably trying to determine whether Ted was a drug crazy or a Mafia henchman. Luckily, Ted was neither, only a recently released felon.

"So you want to order or what?" Benjie said, not waiting for introductions. I glanced at Ted. "Have you eaten?"

"Not yet."

Benjie's eyes moved to mine. "I have a nice blackened grouper."

"Is it hot?"

"Cajun hot."

I looked at Ted. "You like hot, spicy food?"

"Sure."

Benjie never used a pad to write things down. I don't know how he remembered who had what, but he did. "I'll bring you a bottle of wine to go with it. I have a nice chablis."

After Benjie left, I took a sip of water and looked at Ted. "Lieutenant Jefferson tells me you were trying to get a look at police records today."

He grinned. His eyes looked nearly royal blue with the moon reflecting on the water behind him. He gave me an apologetic smile with just a hint of sensuousness. "Not too smart, huh?"

I looked down at the silverware on the table, vowing to keep this professional. "Nope, not very smart. What did you hope to gain?"

"I don't know. I was desperate. That was before I looked you up."

I nodded, realizing everyone is entitled to one mistake. "If we do end up working together, you better not try anything like that again."

He flushed slightly. "Agreed."

I gave him what I hoped was a stern look. "Do you know a man named Roberto Ramon?"

He shook his head. "No."

I relayed the information I'd read in the files about Mr. Ramon's homicide. "You never heard of him?"

"I may have been questioned about him by the police, but I didn't know who he was. My attorney may have told me about him. I don't exactly remember."

"Did you ever hear Feinstein mention him?"

"No. Feinstein and I only talked business. We didn't mention other people unless they fit in with what we were planning."

"You know that Robert Ramon was the gardener for the Feinsteins."

"Yes."

"You didn't see him around that night you went to see Feinstein, the night his wife was killed?"

"No. It was dark. What would a gardener be doing there then?"

"I don't know, just had to ask."

He stared directly at me. "Everyone believed I was guilty of killing Mrs. Feinstein, now it looks like they believe I murdered Roberto Ramon. Even you."

I looked away, feeling a sliver of guilt that I did indeed wonder if he had. But when I looked back at him, I felt suffused with warmth for the man. I didn't believe he killed Roberto Ramon or Aaron Feinstein. At that point I wasn't sure if it was his good looks which won me over or whether the evidence was so circumstantial, he had to be innocent.

Whichever, I had more information to gather before I could come to any conclusions. We were silent for a moment, watching the surf roll in. Then I turned to him. "Was Feinstein having an affair?"

"Probably. He usually was. Why?"

"A woman called the police just about the time you entered the Feinstein house. It could have been Feinstein's accomplice."

"If he was having an affair, I wouldn't know who with."

"Did you ever see him at his office?"

"Sure."

"Were there any women there?"

"Only his secretary, a willowly blonde. She buzzed around me a while,then left. They could have been lovers. I just don't know."

"Is there anyone else you know of it could have been?"

"Nobody that hated me that much. Except maybe my ex-wife."

I was pleased to hear it was an ex-wife he was talking about, but surprised he said it with such vehemence. "Did your wife know Feinstein?"

"Not that I know of, but Brenda kept a lot of secrets."

Benjie arrived with a bottle of wine and two glasses. He opened it expertly and poured some for Ted to try, then quickly poured mine as if he didn't give a hoot what my companion thought. We sipped our wine and watched the waiter depart.

Turning to Ted, I said, "What kind of a business man was Feinstein?"

"Crooked."

"Then why did you keep doing business with him?"

"I didn't. It was our first venture. When I found out what kind of a guy he was, I tried to get out of it, but I'd already advanced him some money and I didn't want to lose it."

"Too much money to back out?"

"Too much."

"Where did you get it?"

"Some good investments. I bought a failing auto parts business ten years ago and it took off. From that I had money to play with. I had a pretty good sense of the market and did quite well."

I wondered how much of that money he had left. He looked tonight like a wealthy man. Earlier that afternoon he looked like what he was: a man just released from prison. I wasn't even sure why he was seated opposite me that night. By rights, he should have still been in prison, but he must have gotten out on an early release program. Florida prisons were overflowing and the mentality of the parole board seemed to be first in, first out. Felons were not held any longer than petty criminals. It all depended on prison space.

I decided it was time to commit myself. "I don't care what Lieutenant Jefferson thinks or whether the entire police force has convicted you in their minds. I've decided to take you on as a client."

He smiled broadly. "Thanks, I appreciate that."

"Good. Now to more practical matters. I charge thirty-five dollars an hour plus mileage. I won't be working for you exclusively, I have other clients I'm working with right now. I will need at least twelve hundred dollars up front. I'll give you an itemized account every week so you'll know I've been doing my job.

He reached for his wallet. Out of it he took a check. "I've already made one out for you."

He handed it to me and I glanced at it, noting the numbers added up to considerably more than what I'd requested. I quickly tucked it into my pocket. "Confident, aren't we?"

"No, I had it just in case you agreed."

Benjie came up behind Ted with a plate in each hand. He put them down in front of us, then stood waiting. I tasted mine. It was hot and spicy, as advertised. "Great, Benjie, just great," I said.

Benjie's glance slid across the table. Ted nodded. "Tastes really good."

"Not too hot for you, is it?" Benjie asked me.

"No, I love it."

Benjie gave me a half-bow and retreated, satisfied he had done his best. While we ate, we talked about the tennis season and the outrageous price of sneakers. Ted let down his guard a bit and told me about how frightening it had been in prison. Under his cool, handsome surface, he began to show a vulnerable side I liked immensely. When we finished eating, I asked him where he thought I should start. "Feinstein. See if you can get that diary."

"Okay, makes sense. Just what does the diary look like?"

"Small, black with gold trim. I think his initials were monogrammed on it in gold. He went in for flashy things."

I knew that about him. Fast cars, fast women, fast money. That was Aaron Feinstein. "When was the last time you saw the diary?"

"He had it with him the day his wife died, the day I met him in his office. He took it out of his suit pocket and set it on his desk."

"Was his secretary around?"

"Yes."

"What's her name?"

"Olivia, I think. Feinstein didn't exactly introduce us. He treats his employees like servants, ordering them around and never showing any appreciation for what they do."

"I guess I'll talk to Olivia first and see what she has to say. Then we'll play it by ear."

I paid for dinner and we walked out together. He wanted to drive me home, but I didn't trust myself. I watched him pull his BMW out of the parking lot, then walked the few blocks home.

When I got there, my house seemed even lonelier than usual. I gave myself a mental kick for not letting him drive me home, but ethics had prevailed. I never socialize with a client, it makes me too vulnerable. Not that his piercing eyes and handsome looks hadn't already done that. My hand reached for the phone and I almost called him and invited him back for a drink to discuss more details of the case. Then I realized that was the least of what I wanted to talk to him about.

Instead, I poured myself some grapefruit juice and went into my bedroom to sort through the information I'd gathered so far. I make notes on each person I've interviewed in a small loose-leaf notebook. I also make lists and lists of lists of questions I need to find answers to and things I have to check out. Some of my questions require legal answers and for those I have to consult books or authorities. I carry pages of loose-leaf paper with me when I interview people and use them to write up my reports.

When I finished putting down what I'd learned that evening, I looked back at the rest of my notes. I try not to make firm theories so early in a case because it might lead to a self-fulfilling prophesy. It did seem clear there were a number of people who might want to set up Ted Sampson including his ex-wife and Feinstein. For all I knew, Feinstein's secretary might have been his accomplice in the whole matter. Anyone who could lift a heavy object could have bludgeoned Mrs. Feinstein and Roberto Ramon, and that included at least half the population of St. Petersburg.

According to police reports, both victims were hit from the rear. The murderer hadn't had to get involved with the seamier side of killing, watching a victim's face cringe in terror or listening to cries for help. One hit with a brass dolphin or a heavy brick and the victim was at least stunned, if not close to death. Attacking from the rear is a little cowardly, but it does cut down the probabilities of a counterattack and as a result, the possiblity of the killer winding up on a slab in the morgue.

The method also involved less planning and risk than some others. The murderer didn't have to stand in line at the local pharmacy and order sleeping pills or be identified by the clerk in the hardware store for buying rat poison. No registering and then waiting for a permit to buy a gun either.

Knives and guns are tricky. You have to know what you're doing or you could blow your own foot off or end up only maiming your victim. Whoever killed Aaron Feinstein and Roberto Ramon had chosen wisely. There were more than a few loose ends for me to tie up in this case. I noted down the ones that occurred to me before I turned off the midnight oil, did a little yoga to unkink my tight muscles, and then crawled into bed.

CHAPTER FOUR

I had a restless night and I woke up tired and cranky. After a long walk on the beach and some more stretching, I felt pretty good. A shower and breakfast improved my mood considerably. By the time I got to my office, the sun was already beating down mercilessly and the thermometer atop the Fidelity Union Bank registered 88 degrees.

I called Aaron Feinstein's secretary and made an appointment to meet her for lunch. She took the invitation so eagerly, I wondered if she was in financial straits. A visit to my local credit bureau confirmed that she had unpaid bills at a number of the more expensive womens' shops in town. Just to see what else might be motivating her, I went to the county clerk's office and the newspaper morgue to check her out.

Olivia Barton was divorced, lived in a condominium on the Gulf, had no arrest record and had never been sued. Except for her outstanding clothes bills, nothing extraordinary jumped out at me.

I managed to arrive at Feinstein's downtown office with a few minutes to spare. He owned the building. I wasn't impressed. Too much glass and steel with a corner tower that had to be his suite. I took the silent elevator up to the tenth floor and pushed through the massive glass doors. The reception area was meant to be imposing, but its maroon and navy carpeting and sofas were depressing. Even the walls were dark, hung with modern prints that reminded me of a kindergartner's paint splashings. Two anemic ficus trees stood beside the front desk like sentinels.

The receptionist looked to be about twelve and I thought at first she might be on loan from the local middle school. But then the older I get, the younger everyone else looks. She was plump and morose with her hair caught in a rubber band and twisted to the side of her head. It looked painful. She wore two silver earrings on each ear and a silver cross around her neck.

She also wore a black polyester suit and a high-collared white blouse which I suppose meant she was trying to look older and more sophisticated. When she opened her mouth to speak, she contradicted her fashion efforts. Her words came out in a high, squeaky voice.

Yet, for someone with the name of Rebecca, she was chatty in a depressing sort of way, commenting on the economy and how her father had been out of work for twenty-eight weeks and giving me a rundown on how many businesses had filed for bankruptcy. She told me this was her seventh month at Feinstein's law office, but she had previously been employed at Richards & Richards, a prestigious law firm down the street. Her fiancé, Ronald, worked for an advertising firm and had a nifty title, but still only earned the minimum wage, so it was imperative she keep this job.

Rebecca had nothing but kudos for Mr. Feinstein and Ms. Barton, but I think I read more than a little dishonesty behind those brown eyes of hers. Or maybe it was fear that she might be fired if she even hinted all was not well at the firm.

As if on cue, Olivia Barton appeared from behind yet another set of glass doors. I assumed she was Aaron Feinstein's secretary from Ted's description. She was a tall willowy blonde who walked as if she might have once been a model. She wore a powder blue linen dress. Pearls hung from around her alabaster neck and crinkled gold earrings decorated her tiny lobes. Her face was made up to look natural and contained all the elements necessary for Western beauty: full lips, high cheekbones, extraordinary eyes and perfect teeth. Above her high pumps, her long legs looked sensational. She was the kind of woman that made you want to go out immediately and have a complete makeover.

My glance went back to her violet eyes. They were coolly aloof, but troubled. She needed help. I look to find something appealing about everyone and I'm a sucker for the downtrodden. She tried to smile, but it was a grim attempt. Her voice was husky, low, Southern. "Ms. Franco?" she said, dismissing Rebecca by not even acknowledging her presence.

"Yes. Are you ready to go?"

She opened a drawer in a cabinet, and being careful not to disturb the dark red polish on her fingernails, withdrew a black leather bag and strode toward me. "Absolutely." I caught a whiff of her expensive perfume. She was wearing too much, as if to tell the world she could afford it.

We drove to Cafe Madrid. I figured I could at least treat her to a nice meal. Correction, Ted Sampson, could at least treat her to a nice meal, in exchange for some useful information.

Known for the best pork chops in the state of Florida, I thought Cafe Madrid might be just impressive enough to get her to tell me what I needed to know. The restaurant is an elegant exercise in design with a fine scattering of antiques and accent pieces, a teal and ivory interior and a discretely-lit fountain in the center of the main dining room.

The super-solicitous waiters bustled around in red jackets, bringing out baskets of fresh bread and sangria. They buzzed around our table with more than the usual amount of attention, but then Olivia probably had that effect on men. She relaxed back into the cushy banquette, loving every minute of it. Before I could start pumping her for information, menus appeared and she studied hers diligently before saying, "I always have the stuffed shrimp."

"Oh?" I said staring at the prices. Even though I wasn't paying, the numbers made me feel slightly dizzy.

Her face took on a sheen as if she was describing the most sensual experience in her life. "Yes, I'm going to get the ones wrapped in bacon. Or maybe I should have the ones in orange-mustard sauce. Both are so good. And the bean soup here is the best, although the caldo gallego is a very good starter, too." Her eyes lit up. "So many choices, aren't there?"

"Umm. Hmm." I was beginning to think this gal had a food fetish.

She crooked her finger and a waiter appeared, notebook in hand. "We'll have the shrimp." She turned to me and said, "You do want the shrimp, don't you?"

I had no idea. I'd never had the shrimp there. I wasn't used to having a woman order for me and it threw me so much I merely smiled and listened to her take over. She also selected a Spanish wine which made the waiter nod his head vigorously. I could hardly wait to see the check.

When the food arrived, she picked at her shrimp, mostly pushing it around her plate. The wine was another matter. She inhaled a couple glasses of it and then ordered some more. It wasn't until she was on her second Spanish brandy that she started to talk. "Why ever would you go to work for Ted Sampson?" she asked, her violet eyes glazing over from the liquor she'd ingested.

"Because he thinks he was framed for the murder of Mrs. Feinstein and he wants to vindicate himself."

She smiled, a sleepy smile. "He's a great-looking guy, but I wonder if he has all his ducks in a row."

I finished sipping my coffee first. Then I asked her what she meant.

"I hardly think the police are in the business of framing innocent suspects."

"Oh, he doesn't think the police framed him."

"Who, then?"

"That's what I'm trying to find out."

"But how could I possibly help you?"

"You knew him before he went to prison, right?"

"Only vaguely. He came to the office to talk to Mr. Feinstein. We barely spoke."

"That isn't exactly how he remembers it."

She leaned over the table and chuckled. A dirty kind of chuckle. "You know how men are. Born liars."

"Some are. Is that how you'd characterize Ted Sampson?"

"Yes, and I'm probably not the only one."

"What did he lie to you about?"

"His wife for one thing."

"I understand he's divorced."

"But he wasn't when he asked me to come with him to Sanibel for a weekend."

If she only knew him vaguely, why would he ask her to go away with him? Either she was lying about how well she knew him or bragging to me about her ability to seduce.

"How did you get involved with him?"

"I was never that involved with him. He was there, we flirted, simple as that." She paused as though she could say more, but didn't want to. Instead, she took out a gold cigarette case, opened it, and held it out to me.

I shook my head. "No thanks, I gave it up ten years ago."

"Me too, but I always come back. Dirty habit isn't it?"

She was making me change my opinion of Ted Sampson and I didn't like that. I suppose I was a little more nasty than I had to be with my reply. "Yes, smoking is a filthy habit and it also gives you cancer."

She blanched, took a slender black cigarette from the case, but didn't light it. Instead, she closed the cigarette case, put it back in her bag, then set the cigarette down beside her plate. Perhaps she wasn't as tipsy as she looked. At least logic was getting through to her.

She swept a hand over the silkiness of her blonde curls. "So," she said, "what did I say to piss you off?"

I lied. "Nothing, really. Tell me about the diary Mr. Feinstein has." She did a double take. "Diary? Aaron Feinstein? You must be kidding. Diaries are for young, impressionable girls. Aaron Feinstin is lucky if he lifts a pen to sign a check now and then. He dictates almost everything."

"Then he's not a meticulous recordkeeper?"

"Aaron? Why do you think he has me around?"

"You don't know anything about a black diary with gold trim?"

"Nope." Her fingers played with the pearls around her neck and she stared at one of the waiters placing a metal container in front of a customer. "I hear the paella is splendid here. Did you know they have a miniature version for lunch?"

"No, I didn't. Tell me what you remember of that day Ted Sampson came to see your employer."

"Well, it was the day Mrs. Feinstein was murdered, for one thing. What an uproar that caused in the office. Natalie, two receptionists before Rebecca, cried for a full day. She acted as if her own mother had died."

"Did she know Mrs. Feinstein?"

"Only to say hello to. That's why I thought it was so strange."

"Any idea what upset her?"

"I tried to talk to her about it. She mumbled something about her mother being robbed six months before that. She was seeing a therapist for it. Guess Mrs. Feinstein being robbed and then murdered set her off again. Mr. Feinstein had to give her the week off."

"Whatever happened to Natalie?"

She shrugged. "Who knows? They come and they go. I think she moved to New York City. Back home to live with her parents."

"You wouldn't happen to have her address, would you?"

"Nope."

"What's her last name?"

"It was Wood, but she was engaged to be married to some guy from Brooklyn by the name of Donatelli."

I took out a piece of note paper and jotted down the information.

"Natalie Wood?"

She giggled. "I know. I think her mother expected her to be a movie star."

There was little hope of tracking Ms. Wood down, but I was going to give it a try. When I'd tucked the paper away, I tried another tack. "How long have you worked for Aaron Feinstein?"

"Nearly eight years."

"What kind of a boss is he?"

"He has a bad temper, but then don't most bosses? Power corrupts or something like that." She took a final swig of her brandy.

"How does he unleash it?"

"Swears a lot. Fires receptionists."

"But he's never fired you."

"Nope. He knows a good thing when he sees it. I've kept him out of trouble with the IRS for years. That alone is reason to keep me."

"How did you do that?"

"I dig up the records he needs, canceled checks, credit-card receipts, calendars, stuff like that."

"So he's rewarded your faithful service with ongoing employment."

"That's right. In fact, he just gave me a big raise."

I stared at her. If she was making so much money, why did she have outstanding bills? Something just didn't ring true. It also occurred to me that she never did answer my question about Ted and Aaron's meeting on the day of Mrs. Feinstein's death. She was playing with the cigarette, bouncing it against her finger. When I asked her about that day again, she gave me a slightly disgusted look. "Not much happened that day. At least nothing that I know about. Aaron shooed me out of the office and I went back to mine."

"You didn't listen in from your desk?"

She smiled sheepishly. "Actually, I tried, but he turned off the intercom from his end so I couldn't hear a thing."

Now I was getting down to the really difficult questions. You have to be a real nosey type to get ahead in this business and sometimes I have to push myself to ask the more personal information. I took a deep breath and jumped in. "Is Aaron Feinstein connected?"

She laughed, a deep laugh that made two waiters turn expectantly and rush toward us. I waved them away. She grunted softly. "Connected? Aaron? I doubt it, but if he were, it wouldn't be something he'd share with me."

"I suppose not. Do you know Dell Channing?"

"Mrs. Feinstein's lover?"

"Then you do know him?"

"I've only heard about him."

"From who?"

"Mr. Feinstein. He did a pretty good stint of swearing about that man."

"Were you and Mr. Feinstein lovers?"

She straightened her pearls. "Boy, you really do get down to it, don't you?"

"Sorry. I have to ask."

"No, we were not then nor have we ever been lovers. How's that?"

"Fine with me. Just one more tough one. Did you call the police about 8:45 the night Mrs. Feinstein was murdered?"

"Are you kidding? I was deep into my second bottle of wine about 8:30 that night and I wasn't alone, if you get my drift." She snapped her fingers and a waiter bounced up with the check.

CHAPTER FIVE

I stopped back in my office after lunch. I had that vaguely sick feeling I get when I've had wine early in the day and asked too many personal questions. My dad had left a message for me to call him. Either Lieutenant Steve Jefferson had been on the horn to him the moment I left his office or he was psychic. Probably both.

Mike, my ex-husband, had also left a message. I tried him first. I could have walked next door and seen him in person, but I prefer not to. I still get a little mad when I see him and his secretary together. He didn't even have the class to fire her and get a new one after their affair fizzled. He probably figured it wasn't worth breaking in a new one. Life stinks sometimes.

When he picked up the phone, he sounded his usual nasal self. "You owe me one," he said, "and I'm in a real bind." He told me that, knowing I wasn't going to argue about it. I was always helping out helpless males and he took advantage of that whenever he could. I hate it when people know you well enough to push your buttons.

I tried to put on my neutral voice but I didn't succeed. "What do you need now?"

"Joe Latimore is claiming stupendous damages because he fell in a hole outside Krispy Kreme Donuts. I need you to find out if Joe is funnin' us or not."

Mike liked to talk that way. I suppose he thought it was cool or neat or one of those outdated terms he liked to use. I probably shouldn't be too hard on him since I wasn't exactly up to date on the latest slang. Some of it even got recycled. Like cool. That was almost always around somewhere.

"Slip and fall" claims happen all the time. A lot of them are legitimate. Mike was probably going to pay off on this one, he just wanted someone to snoop around and see if Mr. Latimore was trying to swindle the insurance company out of a few bucks, and I was nominated.

Joe Latimore lived in a trailor park up by the garbage incinerator. If anybody needed money, he did. His rusting and barely-standing residence looked as if it had already been hit by lightening or perhaps an Iraqi missile. He'd tried to patch the hole blown in the roof with an old straw basket and some palm fronds. Good luck when it rains again, Joe.

A sign above the dull silver of his Streamliner doorway stated simply: *Welcome*. Dingy purple curtains hung closed at the windows and a pink plastic flamingo decorated the weed strewn lawn. The front door stood half-open and I heard a radio playing polka music inside, but I didn't stop to talk. Instead, I drove out of the park and stopped down the street next to a deli and pulled a pair of sneakers out of my back seat and traded them for the sandals I'd been wearing. Then I took my binoculars out of the glove compartment. I slung them around my neck and hiked until I got to the stand of pines on the other side of the park. I stood behind a tree and stared at Joe's home.

I watched through the binoculars for close to an hour and still no sign of Joe. The postman came and went and no one ventured near the mailbox. By then nature was calling and I scooted into the pine stand, crouched down and relieved myself, hoping no one was doing surveillance on me. One of my female investigator colleagues claims she carries a wide-mouthed bottle for such occasions, but I couldn't bring myself to try. (I can rarely hit the specimen bottle in the gynecologist's office.) The woods seemed a better place to me and I was even doing my bit for recycling.

On the way back to my office, I stopped in the credit bureau again and talked to the pleasant-looking woman who'd helped me before. She has a brother who's a cop in San Francisco and seems to feel a special affinity for me. As a result, she let me sneak into files not meant for the public eye. I asked her to see if a Natalie Wood or Donatelli was in her files. She said she'd get back to me.

The day had not exactly been sterling, but then I expect to spend a lot of time checking and cross-checking. Many times I run into dead ends, but it's my chosen line of work. Besides, I'm my own boss and that's the best part.

When I arrived back at my office, I went over the details of my conversation with Olivia Barton. I knew I'd probably have to get back to her, but for then I had enough information to fill several pages.

When I finished with my notes, I picked up my national directory of investigators and called one in Manhattan. He agreed to look into Natalie Wood or Natalie Donatelli's whereabouts. He also said he'd get back to me. My experience with this kind of situation is you rarely find the person, but then I have to cover all the bases.

As soon as I hung up, I looked up the phone number of Roberto Ramon. A woman answered. She sounded depressed and tired. I made an appointment to see her in half an hour. She lived on the southside, an easy fifteen minutes from my office.

That left me some time to give my dad a call back and see what form of mental torture he had in mind for me that day. My father is not a bad man, just your usual guilt-inducing, over-protective, know-it-all second generation Italian-American.

His voice sounded sleepy as if I'd woke him from his afternoon nap. "Theresa? Is that you?"

"Yes, dad, it's me." I could just picture him in his leather chair by the television, with his crinkled gray hair (almost bald in front), blunt face wrinkled into thick folds at his eyes and mouth, evening paper sitting on his paunch half-read, voice coming from deep in his bearlike chest.

I remember when I was a kid sitting on his lap, trying to get the foam out from the bottom of his glass. He smelled of beer and Mennen Aftershave. "Theresa," he'd say, "it's not what you know in this life, it's who you know." I never much listened to his little fireside lectures because he was as likely to counter that dictum a few minutes later with a comment like: "Go to school, get an education. It's the one thing that will stand you in good stead." Maybe it was his idea of being open-minded.

At sixty-nine, he wasn't badly preserved. He had hands big enough to nearly cover a small table, thighs like iron and a pretty fair memory. Better than mine if the truth be known, and he was forever reminding me of that fact.

"How come it took you so long to get back to me? Good thing I wasn't an emergency situation over here."

"Good thing. Dad, I have obligations, things to do, places to see, you know, work."

"And does this work include taking advantage of Lieutenant Jefferson?"

I knew the old buzzard was on the wire before my exit tracks had cooled out of his office. There was no sense getting into an argument about checking up on me because I lost it everytime. Instead, I tried, "The question is moot of who was taking advantage of whom. He thinks there's a tie-in to an unsolved homicide."

The laugh. The deep laugh that never failed to warm me inside. "Homicide?" Then a long pause, followed by, "Don't be stupid now and do all the work and let him have all the glory."

"I'm not sure there's going to be any glory. He gave me the information I wanted in exchange for a promise to keep him filled in on what I learn."

"Well, if you need any pointers, just call up your dad. You know I'll be glad to help you."

"Thanks, Dad. I'll remember. Now I've got to---"

"And don't forget to come by Sunday for dinner. Your mother isn't here anymore to cook us her wonderful lasagna, but I've already got the sauce done for the zitis."

"Dad, I'm not going to---"

"No excuses. Your brother and sister are coming from Orlando and they'll expect to see you."

"I'll try Dad, now say goodbye." My father never hung up until he heard the other end click off. If he was talking to my mother, they'd both listen for the other to hang up and it sometimes turned into a fifteen minute stand-off.

He finally murmured goodbye and I hung up. I put some powder in my sandals and put them back on. Sneakers may be worn with a dress in New York, but not in St. Petersburg.

Heading east on Central, I saw the layer of haze hanging over the air far away in what had to be Tampa. It was probably smog, but we never called it that here. Let the L.A. people put down their surroundings, we never will.

Mrs. Ramon lived in a four-unit apartment by the entrance to I-275. It was a ramshackle frame structure that hadn't been painted in years, of a color somewhere between gray and tan. A pitted asphalt driveway extended on the right back to two frame garages with battered doors. A broken swing and teeter-totter set clung to the left side yard. In the front, amid a dry, sandy stand of sickly oaks and pines, Blazing Stars reached skyward with their tiny lavender blooms. A sure sign of fall and the one harbinger of beauty in the neighborhood.

The air smelled of a fire as if someone was burning garbage in their back yard. Somewhere nearby a radio blared with a ball game and inside apartment A, a noisy argument between two adults was going on.

The roof had been patched so many times it looked like a checkerboard. The doors to the two downstairs apartments hung unevenly on their hinges, making me wonder if they had been recently broken into. My eyes followed a rusting stairway up to the second floor. Mrs. Ramon said she was in apartment C, which I presumed required a trip up the steps. They were narrow and they creaked dangerously. Halfway up I almost went back down and put on my sneakers, but decided to brave it.

When I rang the bell, it made a whiney buzzing sound as if I'd offended it. The door was opened by a woman jostling a crying baby on her hip.

"I'm Theresa Franco, the private investigator," I shouted above the little girl's wails.

"Yes?" She patted the diapered bottom below the child's pink dress and the crying stopped as two wide-eyed brown baby eyes stared at me. Two huge tears stood out like liquid crystals on her face and her curly black hair frizzed out around her head like a halo. Tiny gold stubs gleamed on her earlobes and a miniature gold cross clung to the fold in her chubby neck.

I took out my identification and handed it to the woman. She took it and studied it for a moment as if English was not her first language. While she rocked the baby and stared at the card, I took an inventory of her.

She was in her mid-fifties. Her graying black hair cut short and bunching out unevenly, giving her a tousled look. Dark, nearly black eyes, peered at me. No makeup covered her brown skin, so a small mole on the right side of her nose glowed back at me. Tortuous blue veins rose up her bare legs so thickly, I wondered if they were painful.

On her feet were the kind of fuzzy pink slippers I used to wear as a kid, except the toes on hers were cut out, revealing chipped red nail polish on her toes and two gigantic bunions. She wore a flowered house dress of greens and blues. She was at least fifty pounds overweight with most of it packed around her arms, chin and waist.

"Señora, you call?" she said finally in a Spanish accent, returning my card.

"Yes."

She made no move to let me inside. "You come about Roberto."

"Yes. I'm trying to find out who killed him."

She considered my words for a moment, studied my face, then stood back, allowing me to enter. The screen door slammed shut behind us with a bang. I picked my way across the faded gray linoleum floor behind her, stepping over piles of the cardboard boxes and around the overabundance of dark furniture that had to have come from the Salvation Army. I know because I've found a few good pieces there myself.

The room smelled of fresh laundry, steam and hot metal. A man's half-pressed shirt lay next to a very old iron on a rickety ironing board in the center of the room. A basket of sprinkled clothes stood nearby. Finished garments hung neatly on a rack beside a window.

In one corner atop an end table, some rosaries and a statue of the Virgin Mary arranged themselves into a small shrine while a color television blared a game show at us from another corner. The contestant wasn't sure whether to go through door number one or not.

Mrs. Ramon held onto the little girl's arm and let her slip down to the floor and crawl away. Then she returned to her ironing board, easing her big body behind it. "I got to do these or no money for the rent."

I nodded, seeing her life was not an easy one. Despite the depressing conditions, the little girl was squealing with delight, having found a one-armed rubber doll in the corner. I turned back toward Mrs. Ramon. "Is she yours?"

"No, the lady downstairs," Her hands ran over the white cotton shirt on the board, smoothing out the wrinkles before she moved the iron across the fabric expertly. She finished the second sleeve and started on the back of the shirt. "I work for a man uptown. His wife died. He famous. You see him on TV, on the news. He got famous fast, like one day he nothing, the next he famous."

Mrs. Ramon appeared to be talking more to herself than to me. Her voice went on in a distracted tone. Every now and then her face broke into a smile as if she, too, was famous because the man who wore the shirts was. She picked up a plastic bottle and sprayed some liquid onto the cuff. "See, now the shirt she's drying out."

I watched her work. There was something hypnotic about her movements as if she'd done it so many times it took no effort. Across the room the television flickered and from where I stood I could see another contestant and hear the audience scream their approval. The little girl had crawled onto a rug behind a box and was lying on her stomach, sucking her thumb. The iron hissed with steam and Mrs. Ramon hung up another shirt on the rod.

"I ironed Roberto's shirts. Every Saturday I ironed. A man should look nice for work. He appreciate it. He never said, but I knew, I knew." Her eyes misted and she sniffed. "Roberto a fine man. Hard worker."

She sniffed again then glanced at me with a sad look on her face. "You want to see his picture?"

Her smile was so wistful and her voice so full of pride I couldn't resist. "Yes, show me his picture."

She turned the iron down, then waddled away to retrieve her treasure from the bedroom. She studied it before handing it to me. "His wedding to Ana."

He was smiling at the camera, his wavy black hair gleaming in the bright light. His dark eyes were sensual, amused, with lashes so dark they made his eyes stand out. His grin was broad and engaging as if he knew a secret but wasn't going to tell. Even in a ruffled baby blue shirt, royal blue tuxedo and cummerbund, it was easy to see how muscular and slim he was.

When the picture was taken, he couldn't have been more than nineteen or twenty. The plastic cover over the picture was spotted with fingerprints. I wondered over the years how many times his mother had taken it out to look at it.

Ana looked happy too, as if someone had just given her a wonderful present. She was almost as dark as he, with a clear complexion, white teeth, a dimple in each cheek, curly eyelashes and a plump figure. Her thick black hair curled around her round face and then poured over her shoulders. A wedding dress flounced around her, an intricate affair with lacy details on the veil, collar and bodice. She came up only to the bottom of his shoulder, so either he was quite tall or she was petite.

"A nice couple," I said.

"They were. They get along good." She smiled into the picture. "I named Roberto after my father." She turned the iron back on, waited a few seconds, then tested it with a wet finger. She looked back at me. "Roberto was a good man. He never hurt no one. No reason for someone to kill him." She picked up the iron and shoved it across the collar of another shirt, moving it angrily across cotton for a minute or two before she spoke again. "Roberto a good baby. A good man."

"You always called him Roberto?"

"I did. In school they call him Bobby. He didn't like that. He didn't like anybody telling him anything." I could sympathize with that, I didn't like to be given unsolicited advice either. Mrs. Ramon went on, telling me about her son. "He loved outdoors and the birds and trees. Lawn business was good for him." She hung the finished shirt on a hanger and picked up another from the basket.

"I understand he had worked for Mr. Feinstein."

Her lip curled into anger and she spat the words out. "Mr. Big Shot. Yes, Roberto work for him."

"You know Mr. Feinstein?"

"No. I know he never pay Roberto on time." She shook her head. "My son work hard for the man, but he never got his money when he should."

"Who else did Roberto work for?"

"I don't know their names. I only know Mr. Feinstein because police asked me about him."

"What did you tell them?"

She gave me a disgusted look. "Just what I tell you."

"I understand Roberto went up to Tallahassee before he died. He thought someone was after him."

Her eyes clouded over and her mouth tightened again. "I don't know nothing like that. You ask Ana, she thinks so."

"Is she here?"

"She's working. She come back soon."

"Where is Ana working?"

"She clean condos. When my son was alive, they work together. Ana clean the house and Roberto go outside, cut the grass, trim the hedge."

It was hard for me to imagine the pretty young woman who looked so sweet, scrubbing out toilets and emptying waste baskets. But then, money forces most of us to do ridiculous things.

I was about to ask her another question when I saw her face blanch and her fingers move with agitation over the next shirt. "I try to believe he was only sick, away on a trip. Then I realize, he never coming back." Her eyes welled with tears and grief rolled across her, filling the space between us with a bubble of sadness.

Tears came to my eyes too, and I swallowed to push them back. "It's very hard---"

Her eyes started to flutter and her hand moved to her forehead. When her whole body started shaking, I rushed over to help her to the couch. With one arm around her substantial bulk, I used the other to push away a stack of newspapers in the way. She gave me a weak smile, then slumped onto the cushions.

CHAPTER SIX

I was kneeling beside Mrs. Ramon, wiping off her forehead with a rag I found on the table when I heard a female voice call, "Anybody home?" I turned to face Ana. She hadn't changed much from the picture except for a few worry lines around her eyes and mouth. Maybe she'd put on a pound or two, but she still was attractive, even in jeans and a tee-shirt.

Her face formed into an accusatory frown. "And who are you?"

I dropped the rag, stood up, brushed the wrinkles out of my skirt and handed her my identification. I saw then that she couldn't have been more than five feet tall. She wore dark eyebrow pencil and green eye shadow. Her mouth was perfectly encircled in a pale pink lipstick. Even though she'd been out cleaning all day, her clothes looked freshly pressed and the nurses' shoes on her tiny feet had been buffed to a shiny white.

It only took her a second to see who I was and what I was about. Her face registered a hint of contempt. "You working with the police?"

"No, I'm private."

She handed me back my card as if it carried the plague. "Why are you here harrassing my mother-in-law?" She knelt down beside the older woman and talked to her in Spanish for a moment, then she stood up, went into the bathroom and came back with a bottle of pills and a glass. She handed her mother-in-law a tablet and helped her take a few sips of water. The elder Mrs. Ramon revived quickly, sat up slowly and swung her legs over the side. Ana helped her down the hallway and into the bedroom. The door closed softly behind them.

That left me alone among the cardboard boxes with a sleeping child. For an instant I wondered if Ana Ramon was right. Maybe it was the force of her presence or her accusatory tone, or maybe it was just a hint of something buzzing in the back of my brain, but at that moment my reason for being there seemed vaguely bizarre. Ted Sampson had been convicted and served his time, at least some of it. Why bring it all up again?

But I was also a thorough person, someone who grabbed hold of something with the tenacity of a terrier and didn't let go until I was satisfied an investigation was finished. I sat down on the couch and waited, hoping the little girl didn't wake up again and start screaming. It had been a long time since I'd taken care of a young one. My daughter, Emily, didn't trust me with hers unless she was along to supervise.

By the time Ana Ramon came back, I had gained some sense of composure. I put on my best apologetic face and smiled at her. "I know this is an imposition."

I was about to start asking her questions, then I saw she was distracted, only half listening to me. She checked out the little girl who was still sleeping on the floor.

When Ana returned to my part of the room, she looked older, more tired, as if something that happened in the bedroom had aged her. She sat down in a chair by the sofa and held her face in her hands for a minute. When she glanced up at me, she looked better. "Excuse all this. My mother-in-law is sick. Heart disease. She needs an operation."

She surveyed the living room and shook her head. "Listen, forgive the mess in here, I'm moving her out and she's fighting me tooth and nail." She stared at the cardboard containers around her. "Everytime I pack a box, she unpacks it. In her condition, she can't climb the stairs anymore, so she's got to come and live with me. It won't be the best of accommodations, but at least I have a first floor apartment."

The young woman seemed to have a lot of courage. I liked her. Although she didn't say so, I suspected there wasn't any money to pay for an operation. Guilt almost made me get up then and leave, but she sighed softly and said, "Sorry if I was rude, but things are a little hectic around here."

"I'm sorry to be bothering you. It's just that---"

"It's okay. I can't put Ramon to rest until I know everything and if there's more to know, I want to find it out."

"Okay, but I might have to ask you some tough questions."

"That's okay. I've been asking myself a few since he died."

I nodded and took out my notebook. After consulting my notes a minute I said, "I understand the police didn't believe you that your husband was being followed."

"That's right." Ana stood up, stretched and smiled. Then she motioned me to follow her. "Come on in the kitchen. I have to start supper. We can talk there."

The kitchen was as neat as the living room was untidy. The walls were painted a cheery pale yellow and the linoleum floor had been waxed recently. A bowl of apples and bananas sat on a polished table in the center. The stained formica counter had been wiped clean and the sink was empty of dirty dishes. The windowsill held a pot of herbs and a small cactus. New dish towels on the rack proclaimed: *Have a Great Day!*

I sat in a chair by the table and watched Ana make beans and rice for supper. "It's cheap and it's easy," she said. She seemed to enjoy chopping up garlic and then dumping it into the sizzling oil in a big iron pot. "Do you like to cook?"

"Yes, but I don't seem to find much time lately." I knew that was just an excuse. Here was Ana, running her own business, taking care of an ailing mother-in-law, moving, and who knew what else and she was cooking. I only had me to worry about and I usually ate out or grabbed a quick salad or sandwich. The truth was I hated to cook for one person. It seemed such a waste of energy.

Ana's hands worked carefully, cutting up peppers and then stirring them around in the pot while she waited for the rice to come to a boil. Finishing for a minute, she turned to me. "Now what did you want to ask?"

"Mostly about what happened right before your husband left for Tallahassee."

She nodded and poured some black beans and tomatoes into the pepper and garlic mixture. "That was a bad time for Roberto." Her face tightened.

"What happened?"

"I don't know exactly. He tried to keep it from me, but I heard him talking to somebody a few times."

"Do you know who?"

"No, I don't. I wish I did." Her eyes went dull with hatred. "I could have done something about it. As it was, all I could do was hope nothing terrible happened."

"What did you hear Roberto say on the phone?"

"Not much. He muffled his voice and tried to keep the conversation from me. He was always trying to protect me from things. If he would have only told me---" She turned down the stove and came over to sit beside me.

I wanted to say something to comfort her. The best I could manage was, "We can't always control what happens."

"God, don't I know that."

We sat silently for a minute before I said, "What exactly did you hear Roberto saying on the phone?"

"Just that he didn't care, that he wasn't going to say anything to anybody and that he would meet whoever it was later that night."

"Did he?"

"He went out that night."

"Did he tell you what happened when he came home?"

"Not exactly, but I could tell he was afraid. His eyes showed it. He tried to pretend he could handle it, but I knew he couldn't. I'd never seen him so scared."

"I understand he was chased by a truck."

"That came later. The next week. He was coming back from the grocery store and a truck nearly ran him over."

"Big truck?"

"He said it was a black Ford. I told the police that, but they said they couldn't do anything unless I had the license plate number or something. Of course Roberto didn't have it or wouldn't give it to me, so nothing was done."

"Then what happened?"

Sticky fingers reached up and patted my arm. The little girl must have smelled the food and came in to see what was cooking. I reached down and swept her onto my lap. She giggled when I set her on my knee, held her hands and moved my knee up and down, giving her a ride.

Ana smiled. "Angel's a sweetheart. Her mother's a pain, but at least she has a steady job. I don't think my mother's going to be able to watch Angel for much longer."

A minute later the little girl grew tired of my knee and slid down onto the floor. She crawled over to Ana, stood up and clung to her leg with one arm while she sucked her thumb with the other. Ana looked down at her fondly. "She's got a bad kidney and even with that she's a doll. I guess I better feed her something."

Ana opened a cupboard door and took out a can of baby food. "How about this, Angel?" she said.

The baby smiled and took her thumb out of her mouth. Ana whisked her off the floor and deposited her in a high chair in the corner. "You sit there a minute and I'll be right back."

The little girl waited, banging her fist on the tray in front of her. Ana tied a white plastic bib around Angel's neck, pulled a chair around and sat down. Angel got most of the applesauce on her face and in her lap. Ana was patient, pushing the drooling fruit puree back into Angel's mouth and playing airplane with her. When she finished feeding Angel, Ana gave her a bottle and the little girl sucked on the nipple of it contentedly. Ana turned back to me. "Anything else you wanted to know?"

"Did you think someone was trailing your husband?"

"I did. I saw a guy outside a couple of times."

"What did he look like?"

"Tall, muscular, gray hair, handsome. He looked like a movie star. It was hard not to notice him. I guess I wouldn't have if he hadn't been so good-looking."

"Did your husband see him, too."

"He saw someone, but it was at night and he wasn't sure what the guy looked like. After that, he freaked. He called up a friend in Tallahassee. I tried to talk him into going back to the police and asking for help, but he refused. I almost had him talked into it, but then he got another phone call."

"What was that one about?"

"I could only hear Roberto's side. He was being threatened again. I could tell. I grabbed the phone out of his hand and shouted at whoever was there to leave my husband alone."

"Then what happened?"

"Roberto never hit me, but he looked that time like he wanted to. He told me I was stupid and not to get in the middle of things. By then my Latino temper was up. I told him I was already in it. If he was hurting, so was I. He gave me a terrible look, slammed down the phone and went into the bedroom. The next thing I knew he had a bag packed and was on his way out. I tried to stop him, but he wouldn't listen. I almost went with him, but with his mother sick, I didn't dare."

"Husbands can be impossible. Just ask me, I had one once."

We exchanged knowing glances about the intricacies of male-female relationships before I asked her, "Who found your husband?"

"His friend, Jerry. He'd been at work for twelve hours. He came home and found Roberto lying on the living floor. He'd been dead a while."

"Had the bed been slept in?"

"I don't know. The police didn't tell me that and I never asked."

"When was the last time you heard from him?"

"The night before. He called. He sounded desperate and I begged him to come back, but he said he couldn't, it was too dangerous."

"Do you have Jerry's phone number?"

"No. He wouldn't give it to me. Said the less I knew the better."

"Do you know Jerry's last name?"

"Ramirez, I think. I never met the guy. They were friends before I met Roberto."

I made a note to myself to check up on Jerry Ramirez in Tallahassee. I probably wouldn't be able to find him, but it was worth a try. I looked back at Ana. "Did you by any chance know any of your husband's customers besides Mr. Feinstein?"

"Not really. Roberto kept a notebook of his appointments. It's probably in the bedroom at home."

"Maybe you could call me and let me know what's in it. There might be a tie-in to someone else."

"I'll do better than that. I'll put it in the mail to you when I get home. Just give me your address."

I gave her my card and got ready to leave. I had left the hardest question for last and I didn't relish asking it, but as they say, it comes with the territory. "One more thing, Ana." Her eyebrows went up like danger signals and I knew she had probably guessed what was coming. "Did your husband know Mrs. Feinstein?"

"Only because she was the wife of Mr. Feinstein. I know there was some talk about Roberto and Mrs. Feinstein, but it was silly."

"Then as far as you know there was nothing between them."

"Of course not. Whatever else Roberto was, he was true to me."

"What about the key to the Feinstein's house. They found it in your husband's bedroom."

She looked at me without anger. "If he had a key it was part of his job to have it."

"You're sure?"

"I'm sure. Roberto never mixed business with pleasure."

When I left, Ana was holding a giggling Angel. On the way back to my car I wondered who was going to look after the little girl once Mrs. Ramon moved in with her daughter-in-law.

Now there were two books I was looking for: Feinstein's diary and Roberto Ramon's appointment book. This case was already getting too complicated.

CHAPTER SEVEN

Evelyn Rosecki, my landlady, was waiting for me when I got home after visiting the Ramon women. Evelyn was somewhere in her late sixties, but was the kind of woman who preferred not to discuss such things. She dyed her hair a bright red so I had no idea what its original color might have been.

She's very attractive, with her long neck, thick-tufted hair, and queenly carriage. Tall, tan, and lean. She had an exercise bar installed in her living room to keep her in shape. Her eyes are a deep brown, the color of good earth, and they radiate intelligence and endless energy. Her long, artistic fingers taper to glistening carmine nails and her wrists are always full of slender bracelets which make musical accompaniment to her movements.

When I walked up the driveway, she was wearing a gauzy skirt of mauve over her black leotard, black exercise sandals and mauve hair ribbons in her hair. Around her neck she'd tied a lavender cotton bandana. Gold hoop earrings swung from her lobes. I thought she must be hot with all those clothes on since I was sweltering, but her creamy skin looked cool, her face undaunted.

I gave her a weak smile. She looks out for me so I suppose I owed her something. But I was depressed, hot, tired. The last thing I needed was to listen to Evelyn's latest greeting card. At least I thought that was the last thing I needed.

"Roses are red," she began in her tranquil voice which always carried an undertone of the determined. I stopped listening after the first line, but she seemed oblivous, pirouetting around me, then following me into my apartment.

"Evelyn, I'm in no mood for this."

She gave me one of her winning-over smiles, then rubbed my back soothingly.

"Only trying to cheer you up, my dear. You look like you could use a little cheering."

She was right about that. Spending time with the Ramons made me see how lucky I was to have a father who was relatively healthy and had no plans to move in with me. I wondered how I'd cope with an ailing senior in my household.

When Evelyn gave me a withering glance, I recanted. "Okay, I'll listen, but first I have to get out of these shoes and find something to drink."

She shook her red head and the mauve ribbons in it quivered expectantly.

"I have a pitcher of iced tea in my fridge. I'll get it and be back in a minute." With that she flitted out the door, gauzy skirt floating behind.

I took advantage of the time to pull off my clothes and shoes and yank on a pair of shorts and a tee-shirt. Barefoot is always better. It brings a touch of sanity after a day of pavement pounding.

Somehow, after a glass of her tea and a couple of fig bars, she wormed a few details of my newest case out of me. I suppose I was dying to tell someone, and Evelyn was good at keeping secrets.

When I'd finished, having been careful not to mention anything about how handsome Ted Sampson was or that he was a Paul Newman look alike, she jangled her bracelets as if about to make some profound pronouncement. "I suppose," she said, daintily brushing the crumbs from her fig bar onto a plate, "your employer looks like Cary Grant this time."

She gave me one of her sparkling laughs and I felt my face go hot.

"Of course not," I said, trying to defend myself.

"Good. You get entirely too romantic. I've seen some of the men, they in no way resemble the movie stars you think they do."

"Paul Newman," I said dreamily.

"What?"

"He looks like Paul Newman."

She shook her head disparagingly and her mauve ribbons shuddered. "That's what I thought. Off helter-skelter thinking you're some moll in a grade B movie."

"Paul Newman was never in a grade B movie."

"Perhaps not, but that isn't stopping you from going doornail over broomstick."

"I believe the saying is head over heels."

She gave me a sour look. "Whatever. You know what I mean."

"Yes," I said, taking another glass of iced tea, "I know exactly what you mean."

* * *

Living in St. Petersburg is sometimes like being in an overheated room with bright lights. The sun beats down daily and the temperature is 90 degrees five days out of ten. Only in late fall, early spring and during our brief winter are the nights cool. Otherwise, air conditioners drone on day and night. Those not wealthy enough to afford the additional electricity, use fans, or sit outside on their porches if their neighborhood is safe enough.

Usually there is a breeze, especially if you are near the beach or bay. On that morning, the air was still and hot. I could tell we were in for a scorcher as I headed toward Tyrone Boulevard and Brenda Sampson, my client's ex-wife.

I stopped along the way to pick up a bran muffin and a cup of tea. Sometimes simple pleasures are the best, like pulling over under a shady oak near a small park and eating the raisins out of your muffin first. By the time I pulled up to Brenda's Aerobics, it was 9:25. The green fluorescent and sparkle sign in the window announced classes for children, adults, seniors and special groups. I wondered which category Ted Sampson's ex-wife would put me in.

The exercise studio was attached to an optometrist's office near Ninth Avenue, just past the stop light. The stucco building had been painted a bright peach, one wing housing a fabric store with Halloween costumes hanging in the windows and a stuffed monkey pointing to the shop entrance. I pushed my way through the front door of the studio to the accompaniment of "Let's Get Physical." It was ice cold in there, but the aroma was vaguely reminiscient of a high school gym. A tangle of older women in exercise outfits stood around the water fountain talking loudly. I looked out of place in my tan slacks and pink cotton blouse, but I pretended not to notice. The women kept up their chatter about whose exercise video was better but a few eyed me warily as if they thought I might be the latest recruit for their class.

Farther down the hall a glass showcase exhibited aerobic shoes, workout sets, headbands and various paraphernalia of the exercise afficionado. Photographs of people in various exercise movements had been affixed to the wall by someone with a crooked eye. I sympathized with whoever had done it. Mine usually end up slanting left or right, due to gentle nudges from ceiling fans turned up too high.

I glanced in a few of the exercise rooms. In one, chubby toddlers about the size of water hydrants frolicked in red skirts and leggings. In another, a group of very pregnant women were doing cooldown movements and moaning a lot.

I jumped when a voice said, "Can I help you?" I whirled and almost crashed into a Jane Fonda lookalike. She flashed me an obligatory smile. Her brown hair was pulled back and secured with a silk scarf. A brilliant orange workout outfit hugged her slim, muscular body and a bright pink towel hung from her thin neck. She wore no jewelry except a gold watch with a white plastic band. Layers of ripply fuchsia and lobster red socks bulged around her ankles like live things.

Not sure of her last name, I said, "Are you Brenda?"

She glanced into my eyes, smiled, then did a quick take of my body.

Her voice rang with command. "Yes, that's right."

"I'm Theresa Franco, private investigator."

She laughed, her face taking on a look of embarrassment as if I'd caught her in some illegal act. "What could you possibly want with me?" She motioned me to a small exercise room down the hall. It was empty except for the two of us. Glass lined the wall facing the door and thick pink carpet covered the floor. Although the room was air-conditioned, four strategically-placed ceiling fans blew at full tilt.

"You don't mind if I do a few sit-ups, do you?" Before I could answer, she dropped to the floor, lay down on her back, bent her knees, laced her hands behind her head and started crunching her upper body toward her thighs. She did it effortlessly, as if she could do a million or more. The only sound in the room was the whir of the fans and her measured exhalation as she lifted her upper body from the floor.

Feeling slightly foolish standing, I crouched down beside her and took out my notebook. Between curl-ups, she said, "You're from around here, I presume."

"Yes." I dug in my bag, pulled out my I.D. and held it toward her so she could read it. She gave it a quick glance, then nodded. Most people take me as who I say I am without even questioning and that makes me wonder if they accept everyone else on face value, too.

I put my I.D. away and then said, "You used to be married to Ted Sampson."

She stopped mid-air and giggled. "Is that what this is about? Our divorce?"

"Not really. I'm investigating the murder of Mrs. Aaron Feinstein."

A few more curl-ups before she said, "For who?"

"Your ex-husband."

She lay back on the floor and looked up at me through thick eyelashes. "You've got to be kidding."

"I'm not. He thinks he was framed."

"Sure and I'm Roy Rogers."

"The St. Petersburg Police know I'm looking into it and have given their cooperation."

She gave me a sly wink. "Of course."

"What does that mean?"

"It means that unless I miss my bet, Ted has conned them into it."

"I doubt he could do that."

"Don't wage anything on Ted Sampson, Ms. Franco." She went back to her curl-ups and I wondered exactly what she meant. Ex-wives were known to be surly about ex-husbands most of the time. It was the rare divorce that sustained any friendship. Mostly it was anger, suspicion and down-right hatred. I remember reading somewhere that love and hate were two sides of the same coin, and I had learned to believe it.

I looked at Brenda. "You wouldn't mind answering a few questions for me, would you?"

Three thirtyish women wandered in, chatting to one another and doing a few stretches. Brenda jumped to her feet. "I don't mind talking to you, but I have a class in five minutes."

I stood up and gave her my best eye contact gaze. "Maybe we could start and then finish later. I don't want to interrupt your work." She nodded and I consulted my notes before asking, "How long were you two married?"

She wiped her face with the towel although I saw no visible signs she had even stimulated her sweat glands. "Ted and I were together four years. We met at a dinner party. He was very handsome, very charming, all the things that don't matter at all to a successful marriage. Boy, was I naive. He promised a lot and I thought he'd deliver."

"The whole marriage was bad?"

"The honeymoon was great, but after that, things were all down hill. I slowly found out that beneath that charming surface lurked a real bastard." Brenda glanced over at the women milling around the room and smiled at a few. She went on talking, but lowered her voice so they couldn't hear her. "Ted was the classic heel and I was the dutiful wife. What was that Eric Berne used to say about games people play? Ted and I played everyone of them."

"Which was your favorite?"

"Toward the end it was: 'Why don't you, yes but.' No matter what I wanted him to do, he had an excuse. Usually a pretty good one by most people's standards, but I found out he was usually lying."

"How did you find out?"

"If you must know, I hired a person of your persuasion. I knew he was cheating on me, or at least I felt it, but I had to have it confirmed."

"Did you?"

"Yup. I was pretty angry about it, too. I was devastated. Secretly, I didn't want the detective to find out anything. But he did. I was completely unequipped to deal with what he told me. We had a major fight and a couple of days later I started divorce proceedings."

"How long did that take?"

"Longer than I thought it would. He really took me during the divorce. I thought I'd get more than I did."

I glanced around the exercise studio. "You seemed to be doing all right."

"Only to the naked eye. Put on your magnifying glass and my accountant can show you some pretty scary numbers. Besides, it took blood, sweat and tears to make this happen. I did it after the divorce, not before. I fought him tooth and nail in court, but I only came out of it with a small amount of money. That I put into this business." She frowned. "With the economy the way it is, people aren't spending their extra pennies on fitness. They'd rather be flabby and out of shape."

From the looks of most of the women there, they weren't spending their money on food, either. "Ted claims Aaron Feinstein had a diary. He kept track of all important meetings in it and he wants me to find it. You ever heard of it?"

"Another figment of Ted's imagination. He mentioned it to me, too, but I think he's clutching at straws and paying you to find them."

"When did he mention the diary to you?"

"Before he went to jail. I think he was desperate."

"Do you know Aaron Feinstein?"

"Everybody in St. Petersburg knows him."

"No, I mean did you know him."

"We had dinner with him and his wife a couple of times. Ted was trying to wow them with his charm so Aaron would let him into some cushy deal. Ted was always trying to turn people his way."

"How did you and Aaron get along?"

"Okay. He's a bit of a stiff, but nice. His wife was the problem. I'm surprised somebody didn't do her in sooner. She was the grating type. You know the kind. Nothing was good enough for her. She complained about everything, but never lifted a finger to do anything. You should have heard her: the food's cold, too many spices, not cooked enough. She could go on and on, spoiling anyone's appetite."

"If she was that bad, maybe someone else did do her in."

"It's possible."

"What about Aaron Feinstein?"

"I doubt it. He had his own playmate. He only spent the oligatory evening a week with her. The rest of the time he was working or on his own."

"Who was his playmate?"

She colored as if I had embarrassed her, but then again, maybe I was hitting to close to home. "Word was it was his secretary, that blonde beauty with the wicked legs."

"Olivia Barton?"

"She's the one." Her eyes roamed to the far corner of the room and went glassy as if she was remembering something important I didn't want to hear about.

"No kids from the marriage then?"

Her eyes came back to mine. "Nope. I was pregnant once, but I lost it."

Her eyes welled up. "Damn, it still gets to me." She blinked a couple of times, then swallowed. "I really wanted that baby. But he didn't. I think he wanted to celebrate the night he found out he wasn't going to be a daddy after all. What a scumbag."

"Then you think he got his just desserts?"

"Ted? Sure. Exactly why he might have killed her, I don't know, but she was the one playing footsie with him."

"Then you think Ted did it?"

"Probably." She stared out into the hall. "He certainly deserved a few years in the slammer." She yawned and straightened the shoulder of her outfit. "Then again, nobody liked her very much. As I said, she was a real bitch."

"Enough of one to die for it?"

"That I don't know, but I imagine people were probably standing in line to do her in."

"You?"

"Of course not. As far as I was concerned, she could have Ted. I was almost glad to get rid of him once I found out about his evil ways."

"Who else might have wanted to do Mrs. Feinstein in?"

"You want a list?"

"If you have one."

"Let me give it some thought." The rest of the class filed into the room and found a space to exercise in. Someone turned on a tape and Brenda started to stretch to the music.

"Do you think we could talk later?" I mouthed.

She smiled. "Sure, if you're buying. I'm done at six."

"Okay, I'll be back." I started for the door. The class was already warming up, tilting their heads from side to side to the music. As I left the exercise studio, I wondered what else Brenda might know and how much of it she would be willing to share. I also wondered if I could look as good as Brenda did if I spent time in one of her classes.

CHAPTER EIGHT

After I left Brenda's Aerobics, I went to my car phone and called my office for messages. Bud Arritz, the New York investigator I'd hired to find Natalie Wood (or Donatelli) had called. I dialed him and he told me that Natalie Wood had indeed married Anthony Donatelli. They had lived on Bleecker Street for a couple of years while he finished up at NYU, but had left the city a year ago.

Her parents had been killed in a plane crash so Bud had been unable to get any information from them about their daughter. He guessed that they hadn't moved too far and with a little effort, he turned up a request from an upstate credit company showing an application for purchase of a house in Nyack.

I thanked him profusely for his help and told him where to send the bill. He said it would be in the mail and to watch for it. I tried information in Nyack and got their number. After several strange sounding rings I got a message telling me their number had been disconnected. I called Bud up again and gave him the bad news. He said he'd sniff around a bit more and see if he could find out where they had moved.

Considering myself lucky that I'd been given even the slightest lead on where Natalie Donatelli might be, I decided to celebrate right then by taking an early lunch, but changed my mind halfway to the restaurant and instead headed for incinerator land and another look-see at Joe Latimore. If I couldn't track down Natalie, maybe I could at least catch Joe incriminating himself.

The wind was blowing in just the right direction for me to smell the odor of burning garbage. I hadn't been around when they'd chosen the site or I'd have protested then. Maybe some people did, but the powers that be hadn't listened to a few angry Senior Citizens and the poor folks living in the surrounding trailer parks, so the incinerator went up.

A couple of years ago the county decided we were generating entirely too much garbage (even for an incinerator roaring full tilt), what with all the northerners migrating to our state, people having kids, and everyone living longer. Instead of stepping up recycling efforts or heading off consumption, they decided to build another gigantic incinerator next to the old one. It really makes me angry when things are run by seat-of-the-pants managing. Prevention is the only real solution. But politicians always seem to give us solutions that create more problems than they solve.

My dad says I ought to get off my soapbox and do something, and that if I really feel that way I ought to run for office. Maybe I would except I can't stand the phony posturing, endless meetings and corruption. Besides, I'm an action person with high ethics. I'd not last a day in the Florida Legislature. I'd be calling someone a liar or swindler and lose track of why I was there. So, I settle for writing letters to politicians and voting whenever there's an election and hoping my message is at least heard, if not heeded.

I had picketed about the site of the second incinerator. That time a lot of people complained. Some daring fellows from Greenpeace came by, scaled the smoking tower and hung a gigantic banner from it. They also handed out literature on how much toxic material was being spewed into the air by the old one and how cancer rates went up when people inhaled such air. Since then, I haven't heard a thing about a second incinerator, but I suspect those vultures are still circling, trying to figure out how to build the darn thing without us knowing it.

When I drove by Joe Latimore's hacienda, the sign still hung above the dull silver Streamliner welcoming me, but a variegated hibiscus now decorated his stoop and five heather plants stood along the walkway in neat little black pots. Things had changed for Joe and I wanted to know why.

Joe Latimore had been coming out of Krispy Kreme Donuts the day he had fallen and supposedly injured himself for life. He was a forty-five-year-old man who had been unemployed for six months and was not actively looking for another job. Before being fired for fudging the number of hours he worked on the employee time sheet, he had been a clerk at a gas station. He sounded like the kind of guy who might try to cheat an insurance company out of some big bucks.

The waitress at Krispy Kreme Donuts had filled me in on Joe Latimore. He had been coming in for coffee and jelly-filled donuts every morning for months, spending hours kibitzing with the locals, telling Vietnam stories and complaining about government regulations. He'd also hit on a couple of the waitresses, so I assumed he was either single or unhappily married.

Ethel, one of the trustworthy women who works there, referred to him as a "slime ball" when I asked about him. I think I know what she meant.

I parked my car near the pine forest again and got out my binoculars. I leaned out my window, focusing on his mobile home. "Well, I'll be," I said to myself. I had missed it on my drive past his residence, but now I saw that the hole in the roof had been patched. It wasn't exactly a peerless job, but it had to have cost him more than a few bucks. Unless he'd done it himself. Had he taken out his trusty ladder and climbed up there? If he had, he couldn't have been too injured in his fall in front of Krispy Kreme Donuts.

I smiled to myself, realizing I was about to catch good old Joe in a lie. I reached for my camera, then I remembered I was out of film and had forgotten to get any. The drive to the nearest drugstore took about five minutes. The smell in there was somewhere between doctor's office and beauty parlor. A woman was arguing with the pharmacist. I got my film and a bar of black licorice to hold me until lunch. Then I got out of there before a fight ensued.

I was back at my station behind the pines a few minutes later. I'd just got myself settled with binoculars poised on Joe's home when he appeared. He walked with a cane and wore a spongy brace around his hefty neck. Neither of those threw me. I've seen people feign injury before, evading detection for days.

But Mr. Joe wasn't going to get away from me. I trained my lenses on him. "Take your best shot, Big Joe, because I'm gonna get you." He lumbered down his walkway slowly, flinging his feet out in front of him, stubby arm leaning on his cane.

He was wearing a pair of faded plaid shorts, a baby blue short-sleeved shirt, the kind with all the pockets that barbers wear, and black shoes. White socks wove up his spindly legs and he had a paunch the size of a medicine ball. He was unshaven and his greasy, pewter-colored hair hung down nearly to his collar. His substantial nose was red, but I couldn't tell if it was from drink or from spending too much time in the sun. Been crawling around the roof of any Streamliners, Joe?

His thin bloodless lips were mumbling something, but I couldn't make out what. He wore sunglasses, the reflective kind. I hate them because I wonder just what they're supposed to be hiding.

He hobbled out to his mail box and collected what looked like bills and a discount ticket from the local pizzeria. He inspected each piece as if it might bring him luck, then started back inside.

A small, wiry man with a tattoo of a heart on his left arm bounded out of the trailer next door. He had his cigarettes rolled up in the cuff of his tee-shirt, making me think he was a throwback to the fifties. Even his hair was reminiscient of a bygone era with its upswept, well-oiled surface. The small man pointed to the roof of Joe's trailer and it looked as if they were arguing about something, but I couldn't tell what. I thought he might take a swing at Joe, but instead he made an obscene gesture. Before he re-entered his domicile, he turned around a few times to shout some well-chosen, parting words.

I got out of my car and locked my binoculars and other valuables in the trunk, then I yanked my fifties, ultra-teased wig over my hair, dug out my poodle skirt from one of the boxes in my backseat and pulled that on. I didn't bother taking off my slacks, just rolled them up so they couldn't be seen beneath the skirt, except by someone lying face up on the sidewalk when I flounced by. I took out my old saddle shoes, which had seen better days, and put those on. Although I'd be uncomfortably hot, it was worth it.

I always like to look the part, not just a rough facsimile. For good luck, I opened a piece of Double Bubble gum and stuck it in my mouth.

When I was ready, I sauntered over to Mr. Fifties trailer. I practiced blowing bubbles on the way. When I knocked on his door, "Rock Around the Clock" was playing at alarm blast level from his trailer. Mr. Fifties answered in a flash, his face, devoid of humor and tight with the grimness only a bad relationship can bring, thrust forward through the half-opened door.

"Hiya, doll," he said, face softening while he looked me up and down,"Nice skirt," he said.

I blew a bubble and giggled. Had people really been that wacky in the fifties? I doubted it, but I was having too much fun to stop. "I'm in the trailer down the street. The one with the pink bows on the mailbox."

He nodded, looking slightly puzzled. I had no idea if there was such a bird in the trailer park, but this business calls for improvisation. "I'm taking a poll of people in the park."

His face took on a suspicious look as if he'd been taken a few times in his life. He leaned out the door a few more inches and breathed garlic all over me. "What kind of a poll?"

"We're planning a big nostalgia bash and want to know what kind of music people like."

He smiled, showing me a front tooth with a gold crown. He shouted into the trailer, "Turn down that racket, Doris, I'm trying to conduct business here for Pete's sake." The music volume cranked up a notch. He shrugged, gave me a pained expression and stepped outside. "Bill Haley, Elvis Presley, Tess Brewer---you name 'em, I like 'em."

I took out my pad and started to write down the names, trying to look like this was serious stuff. From inside came a howl. "Who is that, Elroy?" It was the voice of a jealous female and I had just set off her danger signal.

He gave me a bovine look. "Better half," he said gesturing toward the trailer.

"Elroy!" Her voice pierced the air and the front door of the trailer came flying open. His wife planted herself, arms akimbo, blue jeans rolled up to her knees and a black tee-shirt that proclaimed: ELVIS LIVES! She was built like a toothbrush, with bristly hair cut in a DA, dangling hoop earrings, and the face of a Pekinese.

"What in the hell are you---?" She stopped in mid-sentence, gave me a she-wolf look and yanked him inside. "We don't buy anything from the Avon lady, thanks anyway," she shouted behind her as she slammed the door shut and shot the bolt into place.

So much for my disguise. I might have fooled him, but I didn't fool her at all. Women are much less gullible about such things.

On the way back to my car, I pulled off my disguise and threw it in the backseat. Then I went back to my office for some lunch. I ordered take-out from a local restaurant. While I waited, I jotted down some notes about my almost-encounter with Joe Latimore. About half an hour later a droopy salad, some soggy crackers and an iced tea arrived. I munched on the tasteless stuff and thought about what to do next.

When I finished eating, I called Dell Channing, Mrs. Feinstein's ex-lover. He didn't answer. George Burns and Gracie Allen did, or at least a recording of someone who sounded a lot like them did. Cute, but not very informative.

I decided to go home and take a long walk on the beach. That sometimes clears my mind. By four o'clock I was in shorts, sandals and a tee-shirt, headed for the beach. Thanks to whoever makes such decisions, Evelyn was out shopping or something and wasn't around to read me any more of her greeting card poems.

I headed across First Street East and down 75th Avenue. Someone was putting a new roof on a bungalow I thought had been condemned. Maybe it was in better shape than it looked. I wished I could say the same thing about the cases I was working on. So far, Joe Latimore had evaded my clever trap and I had caught Ted Sampson in more than one lie.

I took off my sandals when I reached the beach and walked into the surf. The water was cool and refreshing. Some sandpipers thought so, too. They were digging in the sand, looking for crabs. "Early dinner?" I asked them, but they skittered away, their tiny feet moving down the sand so fast they were only a blur.

A few diehards were jogging along the beach. I like to just enjoy looking at the water, splashing through it and sniffing the salty, fishy smell. I plod along the shore, just barely keeping my heart beat fast enough to challenge it.

The bottom of my feet have taken on the consistency of tough leather since I've been walking barefoot on the shells, but who cares? It is the ultimate in foot massage. I rinsed my feet quickly, put my sandals back on and left the beach. Then I chugged back home and took a quick shower. Ready for anything, I called Dell Channing again. This time he answered and told me he could see me in half an hour at the Brown Derby. I threw on some white pants, pulled on a silk blouse and some better sandals and was out the door five minutes later.

CHAPTER NINE

The Brown Derby is difficult to miss. Its form looms off to the side of the Madeira Beach Bridge. The large block structure resembles an enormous square rigged Spanish galleon. It is a place you go for one of two reasons: either you love immense salad bars or you're coming in by boat and don't want to have to wait too long for your martinis. Dell Channing was obviously there for the second reason. The bar is only about fifty feet from the slip pier, and from it he could admire his boat.

I stood under a fragrant oleander awaiting his arrival. "Ms. Franco?" called the tall rugged man with the lean face. His arms moved expertly, tying down his sloop. Dell Channing had a stubborn, arrogant face, but when he smiled and waved at me, pleasure softened his eyes. His upper body wedged into a black tee-shirt while above his gray boat shoes, his muscular legs filled out his white jeans.

I waved back, taking in the height of his sails. I wouldn't have known it was a sloop except that my ex-husband taught me a few things about boats and ships. "A ship is a sea-going vessel, Terry." I hate being called Terry.

"Then what's a boat?" I remembered asking him.

"A boat is a small vessel. If you can put it on a ship, it's a boat." Simple enough answer for a simple-minded man. We were driving by a marina and I remembered pointing to a particular boat, one that looked quite a bit like Dell Channing's. He nodded decisively. "That's a sloop."

"What makes it a sloop instead of just a boat?"

He was so ready to let me know the answer. "A sloop is a fore-and-aft rigged boat with one mast and a single headsail jib."

That was about all I remembered of my exchange about boats with my ex-husband. Why a guy who gets seasick just looking at water knows so much about boats and ships mystifies me. But then Mike always was a trivia buff.

While I tucked away my memories of Mike and his boating lecture, I saw Dell Channing put out a freckled hand to greet me. The muscles on his arms glistened in the late day sun and the red in his hair shone in the light. He had the tan of a sun worshipper and the body to go with it, if you like the brown fox look---sly, quick, competitive. He'd been doing a few too many bench presses to please me, but then some women would be attracted by it. I supposed Mrs. Feinstein was one of them.

He smiled and led me past a line of incredibly expensive boats towards the restaurant. His stride was fluid and purposeful as if he had something in mind and didn't want to be distracted from it. The only words he spoke were, "I thought we'd catch a quick drink in the bar." I nodded, already knowing he was the kind of man who didn't like to be out of sight of his boat for very long.

We stepped inside into a distinctly nautical setting. Smells of beef, seafood and fresh bread wafted in from the dining rooms. The tables in the bar were already full of drinkers. Some were waiting for a spot in the dining room, or maybe looking for some action. I doubted if there would be any of the latter, but then I could be wrong.

Beautifully-done models, old sea prints and antique ship parts graced the bar and walls. A diver's suit glistened behind glass in a corner, giving the illusion of deep sea adventure. Drink glasses hung upside down from a wooden ledge above the bar that resembled the hull of a ship.

Something reminded me of pirates, as if there should be chests full of old coins and jewels glimmering in the corner and maybe a small stage against one wall, with a young woman in pirate getup playing a keyboard and singing chanties. Maybe someone reminiscient of Joni Mitchell, but not too young or too blonde.

We sat at a sturdy table in clear view of the waterway and bridge. A pair of dolphins played in the water, diving and jumping for our entertainment. The room smelled of popcorn and old wood. I would have liked waiters swaggering in skin-tight trousers, high black boots and colorful blouses, perhaps with bandanas wrapped around their heads and a few with eyes patches and hoop earrings. Maybe one could have had a droopy mustache and be serving drinks called Pieces of Eight or Dead Man's Float. Instead, the staff wore tee-shirts and served quart-sized frozen daiquiris and something orange called Grog, containing more kinds of rum than I'd ever tasted.

"Now, what can I help you with?" Dell asked in his gruff voice after we had our drinks.

I chewed on a fish-shaped cracker and studied him. He had gray eyes that missed nothing and could as easily dismiss me as let me into his world. I had to play this carefully.

Mrs. Feinstein was reported to have been a high-strung woman who let no one, man or woman, get the best of her. I decided to try to imitate her style. I gave him a calculating look. "I have to be somewhere by six so maybe you could help me with a few things about Mrs. Feinstein's murder."

He looked a bit surprised as if he'd expected a pick up, not the third degree. His eyes changed to a darker shade and he smiled. "You get right to the point, don't you?"

I took a sip of my chablis. It had an aftertaste as if it had been lying around too long. I looked into Channing's eyes. "Time is valuable. I'm sure you feel that way, too." He nodded and looked as if he was going to say something, but I cut him off. "I understand you and Mrs. Feinstein were lovers."

His eyes flickered, then held my gaze. "That's right."

"Did Mr. Feinstein know about this relationship?"

"Sure he did, but he never did a thing about it."

"Was that what you were looking for, pistols at dawn?"

He threw back his head and broke into laughter. A few seconds later he said, "That would have been fun. Never thought of it. Too bad I didn't."

"What did you think about?"

He twisted in his chair. "I didn't do Laura in if that's what's you're asking. Why would I?"

"You tell me."

"She was my lunch ticket, my free ride. She could introduce me to important people, pick up the check, things like that." Dell Channing finished his drink and signalled for another before he looked back at me. "How long you been working on this?"

"A couple of days."

"Figures. If you think I had anything to do with it, you're crazy."

"Okay, maybe I'm crazy. Convince me someone else might have wanted her dead."

He tilted his head back and peered at me. "You mean besides her old man?"

"Why would he want her dead?"

"He wanted a divorce but she wouldn't give him one."

"This is the 1990s. A woman doesn't need her husband's permission to end a marriage. Neither does a husband."

His fingers tapped on the side of his glass and his mouth twisted wryly. "Uh huh. Unless there's some other hitch."

While the waiter brought Channing another drink, I thought about it. Finally I said, "A pre-nuptial agreement?"

"You got it."

"And if he sues for divorce he loses---"

"A lot of money. Laura was loaded. Her father owns a couple of big banks. Word is Feinstein has gambled most of his business earnings away. What with his bad investments and the recession closing in on him, he was desperate."

"Did Laura tell you that?"

"Yes."

"You believed her."

"Why shouldn't I? I read enough in the paper about him to conclude he wasn't a financial genius. He had some kind of backing, but I think they dropped him when they saw he couldn't carry his side of the bargain."

"Backing?"

Dell Channing glanced around the tables as if he expected a man in a dark suit to open a violin case and shoot him dead. "I take the fifth on that one. You'll have to find out the rest about Feinstein yourself."

"Did you ever see Aaron Feinstein with a diary?"

"Nope, but then I kept out of his way. We didn't exactly see each other at social occasions."

"I suppose you wouldn't. Did Laura ever talk to you about a diary her husband had?"

"No." He eyed me seductively. "We had better things to talk about."

I smiled at him. I'll bet they did. From the sound of him it must have been a Mexican stand-off as to which of them had the bigger ego. I've often wondered how people like that make love. I don't suppose there's much more than lust involved, but then maybe I shouldn't throw stones. I sure hadn't been able to make my marriage last.

"How did you happen to meet Mrs. Feinstein?"

"Charity ball."

He didn't look the dancing type, but I'll bet he met a few rich women there. "How did you manage to get into her good graces?"

"It wasn't difficult. Her husband was never around and she was starving for affection."

"Did you see her the night she died?"

"Nope. I wasn't even in town."

"Very convenient."

He blanched and his voice came out petulant, angry. "I didn't plan it that way if that's what you mean. I was in Orlando doing some business for her."

"What kind of business?"

"She was writing a movie script if you must know and I was going to be her agent. As it turned out, I made that trip for nothing."

"Was the script any good?"

"Your usual violent, sex-filled, empty, one hour and twenty minutes."

"Given the market these days, it should have sold."

"Laura didn't bother with things like characters and setting. She had a plot, but not much else. At least that's what I was told by the script assistant who deigned to meet with me. I couldn't even get a meeting with the higher-ups." Dell Channing rubbed his chin with a knuckle. "I'm sorta glad Laura never found out she had no future as a script writer."

"Where's the script now?"

"In my apartment somewhere. I shoved it in a closet when she died. Didn't have the heart to pursue anything in her memory."

"Maybe I could look at it sometime."

"Sure. Why not?" His left eyebrow rose a fraction. "You got any screen contacts?"

"Maybe." I am not above white lies in the cause of justice although I am constantly nagging myself not to let them grow into anything bigger. "Did Laura have any women friends who might have come to see her the night she died?"

Dell Channing laughed another hearty laugh. "Laura? She didn't have female friends. She was after men, my dear, and there was no time in her busy schedule for gossip on the phone and beauty parlor chitchat."

He consulted his watch. "Time's almost up. Any more questions? You must see by now that I had no reason to kill her. Just the opposite."

"Is that what the police concluded?"

"What police?"

"I understand they talked to you after Mrs. Feinstein was found dead."

"Sure they did. I told them exactly what I told you and that seemed to satisfy them."

I nodded, realizing that if what he said was true, Ted Sampson might have been railroaded. What I needed to do now was find out more about Laura and Aaron Feinstein's pre-nuptial agreement. Something told me I was going to need another disguise real soon.

CHAPTER TEN

I was itching to get into a good disguise and go see Aaron Feinstein, but first I had an appointment with Brenda Sampson and a few other details to attend to. I pulled into the parking lot of Brenda's Aerobics at 6:05. She was standing outside, waiting in a pair of black slacks, patent high heels and a pink blouse that brought out the color in her face. She had on make-up this time and could have easily passed for a movie star.

I rolled down my car window and leaned across the seat. "Crawl in. I'll drive."

She took a look at the interior of my car and said, "Where are we going?"

"Three Palms."

She nodded. "I'll follow you. My car's over there." She pointed to a white Miata convertible and I nodded. No one ever wants to ride in my car.

The restaurant was only a few blocks away. She pulled along side me within seconds of my arrival and parked her car. Grabbing a black leather bag from her seat, she slung it over her shoulder and we trudged toward the entrance. Three Palms is located in northwest St. Petersburg, tucked in back of a large shopping center. In deference to the name, three spindly palms stand watch by the front door. It wasn't the greatest place, but it was close. We went inside and found a table in the cool dark. I didn't trust myself to have another wine on an empty stomach, so I ordered seltzer water. She had a strawberry daiquiri. The things disgusted me, but she seemed to like hers. "How long have you been teaching aerobics?" I asked.

"Too long. Today one of my other instructors didn't show up and I had to take her classes, too. It keeps you in shape, but sometimes it's too much."

We talked for a while about St. Petersburg and the Dome. I let her do most of the work because I wanted to study her and see what it was about her that had attracted Ted in the first place. Not that it was going to help his case in any way. I was just nosey. After two drinks, she brought the conversation back to her ex-husband's case. "What else can I help you with?"

I smiled at Brenda, beginning to like her despite her extreme good looks and the fact she had been married to my client. "I didn't think you'd want to talk to me."

"I suppose Ted told you that. He probably even thinks I had something to do with Mrs. Feingold's death."

"Could be."

"That slime."

Although I felt like defending Ted to her, I stopped myself. It would have ended our conversation prematurely and made it nearly impossible for me to get the information from her I needed. I gritted my teeth and asked, "Who else might have killed Mrs. Feinstein?"

"I've been thinking about that. I'm not sure I can help you there."

"Olivia Barton?"

"Who?"

"Aaron Feinstein's secretary."

"Yeah, right. Her legs are much too good and she probably doesn't even work at it, but I don't think she has the brains to pull something like that off."

I looked at Brenda Sampson and wondered if she really believed brains were needed. I'd seen some pretty gruesome murders that had been done on impulse without any forethought and the victim ended up just as dead.

She took a sip of her drink and popped a couple of peanuts into her mouth. As she munched she stared at a couple near the door who were leaning close and whispering to each other. "Actually, that was catty. I'd really like to talk to Olivia sometime, find out why she thought Laura Feinstein saw anything in Ted."

"You think Olivia would know?"

She nodded. "Olivia and Ted had an affair, too. My investigator turned up information on them." She finished off her second drink and turned bloodshot eyes on me. "That was when I started to have a little fun on my own."

"You had an affair for revenge?"

"Something like that." Brenda motioned to the waiter for a re-fill. When he brought her another, she downed half of it before she said, "It really wasn't revenge. I was hurting and I turned to the first man who was sensitive and caring. It didn't last very long. Both of us realized it was a rebound thing, but it was powerful stuff. I think he was the one who made me see that I didn't have to stay in a bad relationship, that I had options." She paused and stared out the window into the growing darkness. For a second I felt a bond with the woman. Both of us had been through bad marriages and had survived. There ought to be a celebration going on somewhere when that happens.

She gave me a weak smile and continued. "Ted was never very supportive of me. He wanted me to be Mrs. Ted Sampson. The guy I was involved with made me see I could be anything I wanted to be, do anything I wanted to do. For that I'll always be grateful."

"What happened to him?"

"He's still around. I think he's involved with a computer programmer. I guess I couldn't handle the guilt. Ted's good at it. He's a past master. Nothing really bothers him. Cheat a client, so what? Cheat a wife, it's okay, she deserves it. He could rationalize any behavior. Probably still can."

"You still see the guy you had the affair with?"

"Yup. It's funny, we're good friends now, but there's no chemistry involved. Maybe that was just something I drummed up to make myself feel better."

I looked at her and wondered if she was talking about Ted and me, but then how could she know how I felt about her ex-husband? There was no way she could know. I was glad I hadn't had another wine and eventually 'fessed up to her. In my business, I always have to keep my guard up. My clients and suspects can get sloppy and spill their guts. I have to keep most of myself above that. Sort of a cross between a priest and a psychiatrist.

"Did Ted ever find out about the guy you were with?"

Brenda's face turned wary and guarded. "No, why?"

"Maybe he figures in this somewhere."

"No. Definitely not. Why would you say something like that?"

"Did he know Laura Feinstein?"

"I don't think so. Look, I shouldn't have told you. I certainly don't want to cast suspicion on him. He's one of the good guys. He couldn't have had anything to do with Laura's death."

"Why are you so sure?"

"I just am, that's all. You aren't trying to pin Ted's sins on someone else, are you?"

I looked at her and re-played what she'd said in my head. Was I capable of finding someone, anyone, to take the blame so my hero, Ted Sampson, would be exonerated? I'd always prided myself on being so fair, objective, but in this case, I was at the whim of my emotions. It wasn't a pretty sight, me hounding a woman who'd agreed to tell me her life secrets. I took a sip of seltzer. "Look, I'm not here to blame anyone. I'm just trying to do my job."

It sounded wrong even to me. Like a small-time bureaucrat blaming the system for what happens to innocent victims. The kind who says, "It's not my job," when they refuse to help you. Brenda Sampson wasn't paying me to help her, but she was a sister, a human being who had been hurt and who deserved better than what I was giving her. "I'm not going to push you on this, Brenda. Let's just drop this whole line of questioning."

She looked relieved. Even the small lines gathering around her eyes and mouth relaxed. I knew I had to be careful and not blow this contact. She could be enormous help to me but I had to keep my head focused on the right issues.

"Let's get back to Mrs. Feinstein," I said. "Tell me everything you know about her."

She smiled and took a sip of her drink. "That was crazy. Real crazy. You really had me going for a minute. Sorry I got so upset."

"It's okay. I was trying too hard."

"I don't think Laura Feinstein liked anyone. Someone once told me she had been abused as a kid and I think that stayed with her. She didn't trust anybody, man or woman, because of it."

"That kind of thing can leave some pretty deep scars."

"I think she covered it over by being a prize bitch. She wanted to exert power over others the way her father had over her."

"Get the other guy first."

"That was her all right."

"So besides Ted, who hated her?"

"Olivia Barton, I suspect. She's a bit icy, but once she let her mask drop. I was waiting for Ted in Feinstein's outer office and I had a terrible cough. She gave me some cough drops and we started to talk about how men are the worst when they get sick. I told her Ted just lies in bed and shouts for me wait on him. She said women could be just as bad. She told me that she had been working at Aaron's home. Apparently he had been ill too, and couldn't come to the office, but needed some letters to go out. Olivia went there and they were working on some correspondence. Laura Feinstein came in with a hacking cough, demanding to know what they were doing. When Olivia tried to tell her, Laura slapped her and told her to get out of her house. Olivia said Laura probably had a fever, but even so. Can you imagine?"

"You think Olivia killed her over a slap?"

"I don't know. I remember the look on Olivia's face when she told me. Rage and humiliation can drive people to some pretty weird things."

I agreed with her on that, but there was something about the way Brenda was telling me about Olivia that made me wonder if she was telling the truth. "Can you think of anyone else who might have hated Laura Feinstein enough to kill her?"

"As I told you, she was spiteful, but so are a lot of women and they don't get murdered."

"I understand Mrs. Feinstein had more than one affair. Maybe she offended some of their wives or lovers."

Brenda shrugged. "Maybe. I think she was pretty careful to choose men who knew exactly what they were getting into and were discreet. Some of the men weren't attached. Like that Dell Channing. Have you talked to him?"

"Yes. Evidently he was out of town the night Mrs. Feinstein died."

"Couldn't he have hired someone to do it?"

I nodded. "That's a possibility, but is there anyone else you can think of who might have wanted to see her dead?" I didn't tell her there was no motive for Dell Channing to kill Laura Feinstein because I didn't want to get into a discussion of other suspects with her and lose track of what I needed to find out from Brenda.

"There was a guy, I can't remember his name, but the local gossips were yapping about him. I don't have time for such stuff, but the women who come to my center do. You'd be surprised how much news they can feed me between practice routines. It's the only way I find out what's happening."

"Who was this guy?"

She gave me a foggy look. "I'm trying to remember. Barry something.

Barry McDill---McGill---McCloud. That's it---McCloud."

"So what was the gossip?"

"That he was real mad when Laura threw him over for Mr. Musclebound, Dell Channing."

I was surprised to hear her knocking the muscular type since she seemed to be studying for the role of Ms. Muscles herself, but then perhaps self-knowledge was not one of her strong points. "What did you hear about this McCloud fellow?"

Brenda looked around her to see if anyone was listening. I couldn't tell if her paranoia was liquor-related or not. Her voice dropped to a whisper. "That he was part of the organized crime scene."

"Dangerous liaisons?"

"I suspect so, but Laura liked to live on the edge. I think most of her affairs were to provoke Aaron into some kind of brawl."

I stared at Brenda wondering if she was feeding me a lie. Why would Laura want to provoke violence? Something filtered through my brain about abuse victims and how they sometimes seek to replicate earlier violent scenes either because violence is familiar or because they feel they deserve it or because they think it is the only way to deal with the rage and hopelessness they feel.

I had a client like that once. She'd come to me for help in finding her parents. Halfway through the investigation she killed herself. I carried around a load of guilt about that for a long time, thinking I should have been able to prevent it.

I even consulted with a shrink, a friend of mine who's a psychiatric nurse specializing in co-dependency. She sees people who are in a lot of pain from parental abuse, but have submerged what really happened to them. How can you not? Parents are supposed to love and support you, not use you for their own sick reasons. Years later, after abusing themselves with drugs, food or sex, suddenly the real feelings of rage and hopelessness surface and suicide looks like the only way out.

Could Laura Feinstein have staged her own murder? Could it have been a suicide dressed up to look like homicide? It sounded pretty far-fetched, but I couldn't afford to overlook any theories. Or maybe she found out something about this McCloud guy. If he was in organized crime, maybe he had to shut her up.

I wrote down Barry McCloud's name on a piece of notebook paper and paid the drink bill. Amazing how much a few strawberries and little rum can cost.

CHAPTER ELEVEN

Brenda was a little off in the information department. Barry McCloud turned out to be an investment banker who led a double life as an inside trader. He'd been sent to jail a couple of years ago for securities fraud, tax evasion and perjury. Word was he had established a new business and was about to be investigated again for referring his clients to con men, including one or two he'd met in prison who were linked to past frauds.

I got all these juicy tidbits from Mike, my ex-husband, who prides himself on knowing everything about bankers. He always wanted to be one, but the best he could do was insurance broker. I called Mike after I left Three Palms and we had a long conversation about our kids. Despite our differences, we will be forever bound together by our offspring.

Jeff, our son, he announced to me, will receive a new teaching contract in Denver, and our granddaughter, Elizabeth, I told him, is fascinated by the word, no. We reminisced a little about how her mother, our only daughter, still seemed to be afflicted by that peculiarity.

The glow of parental pride soon wore off and we turned to talk of McCloud. After that, I got off the phone as quickly as I could because it was really burning me that Mike should be one-up on me, even if it was only about a banker with a criminal streak.

I was surprised to find Barry McCloud didn't work banker's hours. Even his secretary was in his office, answering the phone in her husky voice. But then it probably takes a lot of extra hours to falsify records and type up letters anouncing phony business offerings. Mr. McCloud surprised me a second time by agreeing to see me in an hour.

I glanced at my watch and decided to make a few phone calls in the meantime. When I checked my messages, I found Ana Ramon had called and I'd gotten a call from Bud Arritz in New York. My fingers danced across the numbers on my car phone as I dialed Ana. Although it would be interesting to find out what had happened to Natalie Donatelli, nee Wood, the appointment book of Roberto Ramon loomed large in my mind as a more important piece of the puzzle.

Ana answered the phone sounding breathless and agitated. "You okay, Ana?"

"It's my mom. She's taken a turn for the worse. I'm packing her up for the hospital right now."

"Sorry to hear that. Can I help?"

"No, we're fine."

I doubted that was true, but I'm not a psychotherapist, even though I try on the role sometimes. "You called?"

"Yeah, I forgot. So much has happened since then."

"Besides your mother?"

"Yeah, but I don't want to go into it."

I heard a siren screaming in the background. "You sure you're all right?"

"It's only the ambulance. I don't have much time to talk, but I wanted you to know that Roberto's appointment book isn't here. The day you were here, I completely forgot that I'd sold Roberto's part of the business and along with it his customer list."

"To whom?"

"Steve Seguendo. He took the weed cutters and lawn mowers, too."

"You have an address and number for Mr. Seguendo?"

She gave it to me and I got off the phone quickly. Finding her husband's appointment book was beginning to sound like a wild goose chase and the whole incident made me wonder if she was telling the truth. Being an investigator has made me pretty paranoid. Most of the people I talk to give me partially or completely false information, but then I have to expect that because I'm digging into their personal lives, things they would prefer to keep secret. Sometimes even from themselves.

The call to Bud Arritz was a bit more promising. Natalie Wood Donatelli was living in Teaneck, New Jersey with her husband. Bud had an address and a working phone number for her. He had an appointment to see her in two days. "What do you want me ask her?" he said.

"Ask her what she was so upset about the day Mrs. Feinstein died."

"Deaths upset people."

"Given, but apparently she was only Mr. Feinstein's secretary and barely knew his wife."

"Okay, maybe there's something there. What else?" I heard his pen scratching across paper as he took notes.

"Ask her if her boss, Mr. Feinstein, had a black diary and if she knows where he kept it."

"Diaries, this sounds like a grade B mystery."

"How you do go on. Just ask, okay?"

"Sure."

"Find out why she left Mr. Feinstein's employ and if she keeps in touch with him."

"Anything else?"

"Just one other thing. Find out if she called the police the night Mrs. Feinstein died."

He whistled. "You think she's going to admit to it if she did?"

"Who knows? People constantly surprise me. The ones I think are going to tell all end up lying to me, and the ones cool as cucumbers end up drinking strawberry daiquiris and spilling everything they know."

"So it's been one of those days, has it?"

"Exactly. Keep in touch." He agreed to get back to me after his meeting with Natalie Wood Donatelli and I hung up. I stopped at a gas station, filled 'er up and took advantage of their unusually clean rest room. While in there, I washed my face and applied my evening make-up: a dab of touch-up from my tube of Cover-Stick Medium under my eyes, some Creme Rouge to my cheeks and a little eyebrow pencil to my brows and eyelids. Satisfied with the result, I combed my hair back from my face and secured it with two pearl combs.

I don't always go to so much trouble, in fact during the day I sometimes don't wear any makeup, but I figured I had to impress Barry McCloud. With just enough time to reach his office driving the speed limit, I left.

Miraculously, a parking place appeared. Downtown St. Petersburg closes up early. I pulled my blue blazer out of the back seat, dusted it off and put it on. A good jacket can make even wrinkled slacks look just fine.

McCloud's office was in the old Detroit Hotel, one of the city's landmarks. It was the first hotel built by city founders Peter Demens and John Williams and was named after Williams' hometown, Detroit. I liked the hotel. Especially the large tamarind and rubber tree in front of it. I'm not usually fond of brick either, believing it belongs up north with roaring fireplaces and snow shovels, but it set off the building with its two wings and center block shopping arcade.

Built in 1888, it stands on Central Avenue, the main street and divider of north from south in St. Petersburg. A detour inside the shopping arcade can be made though the St. Charles Hotel, a restored brick vernacular style commercial building.

The offices of McCloud Securities nestled in a corner between Gretchen's Flowers and The Bicycle Shop. The secretarial suite was empty when I entered Barry McCloud's office. Soft track lighting showed off the small reception area. Healthy-looking plants were arranged artfully on the off-white counter next to a pile of four-color brochures announcing the wonders of McCloud Financial Center. Behind that, a pair of four-drawer lemon file cabinets stood guard. A computer on a side desk was receiving information from a modem far away and clicking out information on a continuous stack of paper. It streamed out of a tiny printer and collected itself neatly in an adjacent basket.

The rest of the rectangular space of the reception area reminded me of an art gallery with its white walls, pastel watercolors and white tile floors. More track lighting showed off the pictures and a block of stiff black sofas. I wondered if I was supposed to take a seat and study the artwork. Before I had a chance to decide, a door beyond me opened and a man stepped out.

Barry McCloud was a short, plump polyp of a man in a dark blue suit, starched white shirt with cuff links, red tie and custom-made shoes. His dark curly hair was clipped short, making his rather large ears stand out from the sides of his head. He wasn't a handsome man, but he had a certain vitality I associate with money and big plans. His brown eyes scrutinized me from behind wire-rimmed glasses. A couple of his chins wagged at me when he said, "Ms. Franco?"

I nodded and stared at him. His wide neck and broad shoulders made me think he might have been a diver or gymnast years ago before he let himself go. There was also something about him that reminded me of my uncle Jim, maybe it was his thick lower lip or his fair skin and soft manner. Despite what I knew about his background, I liked him immediately. Maybe Laura had, too.

He bowed his head, then said, "Please, come into my office."

I followed him down the dimly-lit hall. He exuded an aroma of an aftershave I liked, something manly, but not too spicy. Corporate Takeover, perhaps. He ushered me into a big room furnished almost exclusively in tan leather and mahogany. He took a swivel chair behind the desk and tilted back in it, eyeing me through the bottom of his glasses. His air was watchful, amused, as if he expected me to say something funny.

I sat on the edge of a deep couch and tried to remember what else I'd read about McCloud other than he'd led a double life as an inside trader, racking up $13.7-million in profits by trading on illegal information about corporate takeovers before his arrest. He'd served one year of a two-year prison term before being released. Since then he had been a frequent lecturer on the college circuit, started a consulting firm and collaborated on a book about his experiences. What Americans wouldn't pay good money to read about.

"So you're a private investigator," he said, picking up his phone on the first ring, muttering some numbers into it and then hanging up.

His eyes darted to mine and I realized it was my turn to speak so I said, "That's right."

Barry McCloud gave me a wry smile. "Some people accused me of being a detective myself."

I remembered seeing a piece on him on 60 Minutes. In the segment he claimed he didn't know about past suspicious or illegal behavior of a certain Panamanian company being investigated by the FBI, a once-convicted Reno businessman linked to the Mafia or a Florida company accused of ripping off customers.

I put on my best insider smile and said, "You mean the Associated Press interviewer?"

He was flipping through his phone messages, tossing them into three piles. I wondered which one took priority. He didn't bother to glance up when he said, "That interviewer got it all wrong. People don't hire me to be their detective. They hire me to help structure deals and negotiate on their behalf."

I noticed the look of a money manager growing inside him. His eyes scanned the room, no doubt not wanting to miss anything even vaguely resembling a client should such a person enter his office. Even his hand was twitching, probably in anticipation of picking up the phone and cradling it on his shoulder while talking big business deals.

My attraction for the man was slowly draining out of me. He had seemed interesting and attentive at first, but then I saw it was just a ruse. Once in his office, he wrapped himself up in his work.

I dated a man like that a few years ago. Worse even. He was so consumed with his business he couldn't leave it for even a two-hour date. Our relationship ended quickly when he insisted on taking three calls at our table in the restaurant. I told him he ought to have his phone surgically implanted in his ear so he wouldn't have to interrupt our time together. Completely missing my point, he told me he was getting a new computer, one that would keep him current on everything that was happening while we were having dinner. That was our last date.

When I came back from my visit to the past, I saw Barry McCloud slide his chair over to a glowing computer terminal. His fingers flew over the keyboard, filling the screen with numbers. He stared at them intently, then relaxed back in his chair. He was plugged into his world of wheeler dealing and all was right with his world.

When he finally looked back at me I said, "You'll be happy to hear I'm not at all interested in investments. I'm really more interested in Laura Feinstein."

He gave another quick look at the monitor before he said, "Laura's dead."

"So I heard. I also heard you knew her."

He sniffed, forcing his nose into a position I associate with disgust. His fingers tapped out some more words and numbers rushed onto the screen. "We were acquainted."

"I heard you were intimately acquainted."

He pushed his chair away from the screen and gave me an intimidating look. "What kind of an investigator are you?"

"The private kind." I'm used to staring down intimidating suspects and Barry McCloud was no different.

His fingers tapped on the desk. "Who hired you?"

"Ted Sampson."

"Figures."

"He wants me to find out who really murdered Laura Feinstein. He's tired of having people think it was him."

"What if it was him?"

"Then I suspect he won't be too happy with my report. In the meantime, maybe you can fill me in on the details of your relationship with the deceased."

He sighed and fingered his expensive tie. "It's no secret. Laura and I spent some time together."

"And you were angry when she broke it off."

"Not that angry. Laura could be a controlling bitch when she wanted to be."

"Then what attracted you to her?"

"We were two of a kind. She could manipulate people and situations like nobody else." Barry McCloud smiled to himself. "Except maybe me."

"Word was you two were pretty cozy."

"Probably a little gossip Laura spread around. She liked to do that kind of thing."

"Then you weren't angry when the relationship ended?"

"Only a little. I thought we might have a future together if she'd get rid of that fool Feinstein."

"You don't like Mr. Feinstein?"

"Hell no. He's the worse businessman I ever met. Laura and I used to laugh about the stupid things he was involved in."

"How did you and Laura meet?"

"At a fund-raiser. Laura knew how to draw people around her to get what she wanted. She was one helluva woman at first. I was attracted to her ability to maneuver with the big boys. I'd been up to my ears in business for the past twenty years. Laura showed me the other side of life, the part I had been avoiding through work. I was really sorry we didn't get to know each other better."

"Sorry enough to kill her?"

He whirled his head, eyes riveting on the monitor before his hand crashed down on the desk. I assumed it was in reaction to something he'd seen on his screen, but it might have been to what I'd said. "Don't be silly," he said, his face taking on a nasty look. "Enough people knew about our relationship that it would have been suicidal to seek revenge. Besides I was out of the country the night she died."

"Anyone with you?"

"No, but I was in constant phone communication with my secretary. She can verify it. If I need to have it verified."

I shrugged. "You wouldn't have had to get rid of Mrs. Feinstein yourself."

He lips twisted into a cynical smile. "No, but the police didn't suspect me so why should you?"

"Maybe the police didn't know about you."

"Maybe not."

"I hear you were plenty miffed when Laura took up with Dell Channing."

"Only a little. In this business, you don't have time for much personal life. Rumor built it up to be much more than it was. If I go out once a month that's a lot. Besides, most women won't stand for the constant check-ins I have to do with my computer and phone."

I nodded. At least the Barry McCloud was honest about his lifestyle. I wondered if he was being honest about the rest.

CHAPTER TWELVE

It was nearly ten when I got back from Barry McCloud's office. The moon was creating a silvery effect on the tile roof and the pink stucco front of my house looked nearly purple. A breeze was coming off the Gulf and I could almost smell the sand crabs while I pictured them dancing along the beach.

Evelyn, my landlady, was home. The lights were off, but Tony Bennett was bellowing about leaving his heart in San Francisco and I knew she'd never go out and leave her recorder turned on. I wondered what she was doing alone in there, in the dark. Maybe just listening. Then again, maybe she had company. Although no cars decorated the driveway, someone could have walked over. Like Benjie. I like having fantasies about other people's love lives. It keeps my mind off my own sad, nearly non-existent one.

I stumbled in the door, not sure if I was weak from hunger or fatigue. I threw my bag on the floor by a wicker settee, stepped out of my shoes and headed for the kitchen. I'd try the hunger solution first. I opened the refrigerator door and stared at its bleak contents until the blasts from my Frigidaire cooled the room off. Nothing I saw appealed to me in the least and I slammed the door shut, wondering what I had just added to my already exorbitant electric bill.

I couldn't think of anything that sounded good to eat except chocolate ice cream and I knew I didn't have any of that. I never bought it because I was apt to eat half a gallon of the stuff if I left it hanging around. I knew I needed something nourishing, but the only things I could stomach were cereal and fruit. I took a browning banana out of a wicker basket and sliced it into a bowl on top of a mound of uncooked oatmeal. A few spoonfuls of yogurt and honey made it taste pretty good. Good enough to have two helpings of the stuff, standing at my kitchen counter. I finished off with a multi-vitamin and two mineral tablets. My brain kicked into working phase about ten minutes later when it started to analyze the information I'd picked up since Ted Sampson had hired me. A lot of it was contradictory, but I concluded I needed to ask my client a few more questions before I went to see Aaron Feinstein.

Or maybe I was just lonely and wanted to see a handsome man that night. Whichever, when I called him, he offered to meet me at the Tiki Bar. I'd almost invited him over to my place, but I make it a rule never to have clients there. If there would ever be an exception, Ted would have been it, but for the time being at least, I didn't weaken.

The customers under the thatched roof had been drinking for hours and a few young men dressed in jeans and tee-shirts were talking loudly and looking down over the wrought iron fence as if there might be something there to see. I didn't bother trying to find out. I saw Ted's lean frame at a table in the moonlight and marched right over to him.

The singer, a tall, skinny guy in a Hawaiian shirt and white shorts was belting out "Runaway," and the few couples at the surrounding tables were singing along with him in their off-key voices. The pool was deserted, but someone had left a really ugly striped towel on one of the lounge chairs. Although it was late, the smell of frying food mingled with the salt air. Benjie wasn't around so I figured he was off for the night.

Ted was wearing a white short-sleeved shirt and jeans. It looked as if he'd gotten a little more tan since I'd last seen him and he'd had his hair cut, too. But it was the same wonderful face and those eyes of his gave me a seductive look when I sat down in the chair opposite him. I would have taken the one next to him, but I didn't trust myself. Moonlight over the Gulf and the company of a handsome man could put me in an amorous mood, but I didn't want Ted to know that.

I took out my notebook and tried to look officious. The waiter came by and stood in front of me, waiting. I wasn't sure what the appropriate after dinner drink was for cereal and bananas so I played it safe and ordered seltzer water.

Ted leaned back in his chair and looked at me. "How's it going?"

"Pretty much the usual."

"What have you found out?"

"That you haven't told me everything."

He gave me a broad smile, the kind that make leading ladies collapse into their leading man's arms. "I don't know everything. That's why I hired you."

I looked away, furious I was having such a predictable reaction to him. I stared at an overweight man in tight shorts waddling down the steps to the beach, knowing that would take some of the romance out of my soul. When I had myself better in hand, I turned to Ted and said, "Do you know anything about a pre-nuptial agreement between Laura Feinstein and her husband?"

He smiled at me, an infectious grin that made me want to smile back. "No, I don't know of any pre-nuptial agreement, but why would I? It's not the kind of thing people discuss."

I nodded. "I suppose not." He was making sense and that bothered me, too. Everything about him bothered me.

He took a sip of his drink, then said, "Who have you been talking to?" I told him about my conversation with Olivia Barton. He shook his head. "She's a strange woman. I'll bet Feinstein put her up to making it seem like I was after her."

It was possible, but then why did I have that queasy feeling in my stomach I sometimes get when someone lies to me? I suppose it could have been from too much cereal and bananas, but I doubted it. "Why would Feinstein want to do that?"

Ted shrugged. "To discredit me. Why did he do half of what he did? To cover his ass about his wife's murder." His face tensed, creating a defiant look to his features. "You haven't talked to him about all this, have you?"

I shook my head. "No."

"You aren't going to, are you?"

I waffled. "I'm not sure." Just like my clients don't tell me everything, when I'm working on an investigation, I don't tell them everything either. I used to, but I found out that they sometimes screw up my moves if they know too much. I took a sip of seltzer and waited. Finally I said, "Did Laura Feinstein have any reason to commit suicide?"

He answered immediately. "Of course not. She had everything to live for. Besides, she was hit from behind, wasn't she?"

"Yes, but things can be arranged---"

"You're kidding."

I wasn't. I once had a client who arranged his own death. It was unusual, but not impossible. Sometimes people don't have the guts to kill themselves directly, but can either pay someone else to do the job or set up a situation so they are killed.

He took a sip of his beer and said, "That sounds like movie stuff."

"Perhaps, but I've seen it happen."

"Okay, but Laura wasn't like that. She had deals to plan, people to control. She wouldn't have killed herself or hired anyone to do it."

"You may be right. If that was the case, wouldn't it make sense that she had some kind of pre-nuptial agreement with Feinstein?"

"I guess so. She was one lady who knew how to take care of herself. She wasn't about to let anyone take advantage of her. Especially not a husband."

"But you never actually heard about such an agreement."

"No, but it must be in her papers."

"Who was her lawyer?"

"That I don't know."

"Was she writing a screenplay?"

"What?" Ted's face became more animated again, pulling into an irresistible grin. "Screenplay? Laura? I don't think so, she never told me about it, but then she probably had a lot of things going I knew nothing about." The grin turned ugly, like a warning cloud in a perfect sky.

"What kinds of things was Laura involved in?"

"That's just it. I don't know." His face closed over, becoming unreadable. He leaned back in his chair and crossed his arms. "Another reason I hired you."

I wasn't sure whether he was lying to me or not and the thing that bothered me about that was I had no way to find out. I took another sip of my drink and said, "I spoke with Mrs. Ramon, the widow of Roberto Ramon."

He gave me a strange look I couldn't decipher and I went on. "She said she saw a man answering your description outside her house right before her husband was killed."

"People say a lot of things."

I was beginning to feel he was toying with me, but I plodded on. What else could I do? He was my client and he was paying me. I decided to take a firmer hold on the proceedings. "Cut the crap, was it you Mrs. Ramon saw?"

He nodded, looking a bit startled at my word choice. "Sure she saw me. I saw her, too."

I almost didn't want to know the answer to my next question, but I had to ask it. I turned to him and said, "What were you doing there?"

"Feinstein sent me there. He gave me the address and told me to check it out as a possible site for a warehouse for the printing company I was going to invest in."

"You didn't think it was strange there was a house on the lot?"

"Not really. Feinstein told me it was condemned and that they were tearing it down."

It seemed unlikely, but possible. In my business, I work on probabilities, not foregone conclusions. I consulted my notepad for a few minutes, but couldn't or wouldn't find any more questions to ask. I left him sitting in his chair, smiling. I didn't like him as much as I had before, but I was still under his seductive spell. I could see how Laura and Olivia must have felt. I didn't know any more than before, yet for some reason I blamed myself, not him, for my dilemma.

CHAPTER THIRTEEN

The next day I woke up to a cloudy sky and a storm brewing off the Gulf. When I'd gone to sleep, a warm breeze had been blowing in my bedroom window. Overnight, the breeze had turned humid and cool. I rolled out of bed and pulled on a pair of sweatpants and a long cotton shirt. Then I did a few stretches and hurried toward the beach, hoping to get a walk before the rain began.

Living in Florida, I'm spoiled. For some reason I expect sunshine 365 days a year. I only get it about 360 days. When I don't see the sun for a day, I feel depressed and low on energy. A brisk walk can remedy that most of the time.

My sneakers padded along the asphalt down First Street East and across Gulf Boulevard. The malamute puppy who's often tied outside his owner's house didn't even come out to greet me. I figured he wasn't stupid enough to be outside when lightning was already sparking through the sky over the water.

I only met one other walker, a tall man with a determined look on his face and no spare flab on his body. The joggers had stayed in that morning. The surf was churning unusually high for the Gulf and it was a turgid brown with white foam. Some fishy seaweeed had been strewn on the shore, making an unappetizing sight. Perhaps that's why even the birds hadn't come out for their seafood breakfasts.

Thunder rumbled out at sea and I picked up my pace. My mind was circling around the Ted Sampson case until I remembered I hadn't done much about checking out Joe Latimore's injuries. I made a mental note to get my tail up there as soon as I'd showered, eaten and dressed. After that, I'd make a little visit to Aaron Feinstein's office.

I got back home just as the rain started. I thought that might be a good omen, but I was wrong. I tipped over the blender and spilled protein drink all over my counter. The pants I pulled on had a broken zipper and I had to pick through my closet to find another pair. Skirts just aren't conducive to crawling in and out of a car twenty times a day, nor do they flatter my less than perfect legs, so I usually end up in pants. Unfortunately, I hadn't done my wash for more than a week and my clothing choices were narrowed considerably. I made another mental note, this time to throw in a load of wash that evening. I finally settled for a pair of apricot rami and cotton pants, a long sleeve white cotton shirt and beige flats.

The rain had slowed to a mist by the time I pulled into the trailer park. I took up my usual position in the stand of pines and stared through my binoculars. Someone had removed the dingy purple curtains in Joe Latimore's silver

Streamliner and put up some revolting green ones, the same color as an army blanket.

A dilapidated maroon station wagon with fake wood panels and an NRA sticker pulled up in front of the Streamliner and honked. Joe hobbled out, slammed the door of his trailer shut and hurried toward the car, maneuvering pretty well with his cane for someone claiming he'd been maimed for life in an accident.

I jumped in my car and headed for the entrance to the park, figuring I'd follow them and see where they were going. I waited behind a billboard for close to three minutes before I figured out there was another exit. I roared into the trailer park and took the most likely road, a wide concrete expanse. Not far along it, I saw black exhaust and then the maroon station wagon.

It was jolting and shimmying across the road as if it had no shocks at all. Either that or its driver had no idea what he was doing. The station wagon screeched off the dirt lane and onto the asphalt road behind the park. I followed, I hoped at a discreet distance.

After pulling into a gas station for a fill up, the station wagon continued, in the direction of the beach. I must have been careless or just had bad luck because at the next red light, I was left behind a VW bug that flooded.

Somehow I wasn't that bothered by the whole thing. Maybe I was just interested in getting on with Ted Sampson's case. By then, the sun had come out, drying the few puddles in minutes. Since the ground in St. Petersburg is mostly sand, water drains through it like a sieve.

When a call came through on my car phone, I pulled over under a shady tree by a bus stop and chatted with Bud Arritz. He'd been in touch with Natalie Wood-Donatelli, Aaron Feinstein's ex-receptionist, in Teaneck, New Jersey.

"What did you find out?" I asked, making notes as we spoke.

"She wasn't too happy to see me. I'm not even sure if she's telling the truth."

"What else is new?"

We both laughed, then he said, "She claims she was upset when Mrs. Feinstein died because she'd known the woman pretty well. Apparently Mrs. Feinstein came in the office a lot to see her husband and the two of them became friends."

"Did she say anything else?"

"She says she never saw a black diary, but he could have had one. He was a secretive man, she says, one who was apt to keep things like that from her."

"Did she sound convincing?"

"Yes, but you know people sometimes fabricate the truth to fit with their own sense of what happened. She said she left Mr. Feinstein's employ because he refused to give her the pension he had promised. He had invested the money that was supposed to go in her account on some real estate deal."

"I can believe that. Aaron Feinstein is not known for his high morals. What about calling the police the night Mrs. Feinstein died?"

"She said she would never do something like that, that she was with her fiancé and that he can vouch for it if he has to. I told her I didn't think it would come to that." Bud paused and waited. "It won't, will it?"

"Not from me, but the police here might be interested. Lieutenant Jefferson didn't let me look at the files out of the kindness of his heart. He's going to want some information pretty soon."

I must have been psychic, because no sooner did I hang up the phone but a call came in from my father. Could I meet him for lunch. Very important. He wouldn't take no for an answer, not that I wanted to give it to him. I was confused and frustrated and needed some direction. My father might be able to give me an objective opinion on where the Ted Sampson case was going. He'd helped me clear my mind before and it was certainly worth a try.

I checked my watch and found I had an hour to kill. Steve Sequendo was still on my mind. If he had Roberto Ramon's list of clients, I might be able to find out something to blow open this case. So far it was limping along like Joe Latimore, able to do much more than it was showing, but keeping a tight cover on its important motives.

While I drove to Steve's house, I thought about what Bud Arritz had told me. At a red light, I pulled out my notebook. Just as I had thought, Olivia Barton told me Natalie Wood-Donatelli barely knew Mrs. Feinstein. But Bud told me they were friends. Who was lying? My bet was Olivia.

I didn't trust perfect-looking women. Mike says I'm just jealous. It's true I think things come to easily for them because of their looks. That can lead them into some pretty unethical situations. On second thought, maybe I was jealous. But then, why did Olivia lie? It brought me back to Aaron Feinstein. Was she covering for him as Ted Sampson claimed? If so, maybe Ted was right: Aaron Feinstein may have set him up. I felt a swell of trust for Ted again. It's always easier when you like your clients. Not as much as I liked mine, but at least enough to trust 80 percent of what they say.

Steve Sequendo lived in a condo near the Tyrone Mall. I always wondered if I'd dress better if I was within walking distance of a couple of womens' stores. The answer is probably no. I take pride in shopping sales and discount houses, finding the cheapest version of whatever I want. Sometimes that turns out to be not the best made or most flattering, but so be it. I refuse to be a victim of Madison Avenue's dictates.

The sprinkler system was sending jets of reclaimed water across the closely clipped grass of Steve Sequendo's condo complex. It smelled like rotten eggs or worse, but it was a cheap way of watering. In Florida, with water in short supply, some people claim it is the way to go. I prefer to let the rains take care of the grass. If it doesn't rain, too bad. Maybe God didn't mean us to be mowing the pesky stuff anyway. I'd rather have wild flowers and knee-high grass than pesticides, fungicides, mowers and sprinkler systems, especially if it means having drinking water a couple of years down the road.

Four three-story buildings made up the condo complex. They were all a pale yellow stucco with screened porches and black window frames punctuating the square boxed residences. The white tile roofs needed bleaching, otherwise it looked to be a well-kept complex. Oleanders pruned into trees added splashes of shocking pink and the heather groundcover had grown thick with purple blooms.

I pulled in the driveway and drove along the narrow street past two green clay tennis courts and an olympic-size pool. A few sun worshippers stretched out on white chaise longues, their sunscreened faces turned upwards toward the blazing sun, probable victims of sun cancer and wrinkles in a few years, but having a ball now enjoying their leisure.

I spotted Steve Sequendo's condo and parked in front of the building. A black truck sported two magnetic signs reading: *AAA Lawn and Tree Service, 32l-084l.* I was surprised somebody hadn't stolen the signs yet, but then it was a pretty good neighborhood.

The front door stood open, revealing a tightly closed black metal screen door that let in breezes, but kept out insects and intruders. I pushed the bell by the side of the door and waited. "Be right there."

It was a woman's voice with a definite Spanish accent.

She came sauntering toward me down a long hall, her sandaled feet making little click-clacks across the tile floor. She was of medium height and heavy build with dark hair chiseled into thick braids. She wore a striped cotton T-dress in green and white that reminded me of an awning I'd seen somewhere. Her face contained the remnants of teenage acne, but her perfect white teeth dazzled me with a radiant smile. "Yes?" she said. I showed her my ID through the screen. Her smile faded and her brown eyes glowed with fear. "Is it Xavier again?"

"No, it's about Steve Sequendo."

"Steve?" She touched her wedding band and her dark eyes flashed. "What about Steve?" Her voice had taken on a surly tone and she looked at me as if I might be trying to snatch a prize husband away from her.

"He hasn't done anything bad or anything like that. Could I come in and talk to you? It's about Roberto Ramon's death." When she didn't budge, I introduced myself.

"I'm Isabel, Steve's wife," she said, her eyes turning contemplative before she slipped the latch and let me in. She slammed the screen door locked, then whisked in front of me, moving past a neat kitchen with her skirt wafting behind. I followed, snooping into each doorway when I got the chance. It looked like two bedrooms, two baths.

Steve Sequendo was doing pretty well for himself. A lot of the lawn and tree services I'd heard about went into business on a wing and a prayer and lasted a year or less. With his truck parked in front, I wondered who was cutting lawns.

The place was done in dark, heavy furniture and red carpeting. The smell of mildew was everywhere and I thought I detected a faint odor of animal urine, but there was no sign of a pet.

Sliding glass doors on one side of the living room opened out onto the screened in porch. She stopped just short of it in the living room, plopped down on a low couch and motioned me to sit. Before I had adjusted my body on the lumpy cushion, she offered me a box of chocolates. When I refused, she took two out and set them down in front of her. I looked at her braids, envying of their thickness.

She tore her eyes from the sweets. "How do you know Steve?"

"I don't know him. Mrs. Ramon, Roberto's widow, said she sold the lawn part of her husband's business to Steve."

"Yes." She wiped her wedding band across her skirt as if she'd dirtied it. "My husband bought the business. It hasn't been any great success." Her thick lips pouted for a second, then she reached down and popped one of the chocolates into her mouth. She licked each of her stubby fingers, then chewed contentedly before swallowing. She half winked at me. "If I don't have chocolate everyday I feel terrible."

I had a sister-in-law like that. Betsy marvelled that I never ate chocolate even though it didn't agree with me. "How do you manage? I mean chocolate is just the greatest." I supposed Betsy and Isabel Sequendo would would get along famously, sharing chocolate recipes and eating chocolate candy together.

I changed the subject. "Is your husband here?"

She shook her head. "He went out with his brother to buy a lottery ticket. He hopes to win the thirty million dollars."

"Him and about thirty million other people." She didn't get the joke.

I don't gamble myself and have a hard time understanding those who do. Even when I was married and went to an insurance convention in Los Vegas with Mike, I wasn't tempted. I enjoyed the pool, the tennis courts and the great food. Spending money on a lottery ticket that guarantees you a one in twenty-five million chance, about the same as being struck by lightning, seems like a waste.

I watched her stare at the candy in front of her, then said, "I don't suppose you know if your husband has the list of customers that came with the business?"

"What list?" she said, eyeing the second piece of chocolate.

"The one Mrs. Ramon says she gave you."

She nodded. "That list. Yes, he got it, but he doesn't have it anymore."

"What happened to it?"

"It wasn't any good. The people on it either had their own lawn services or had gone out of business."

"Do you remember any of the names."

She consulted the ceiling as if the answer might be there. She moved her tongue over her teeth, probably searching for the last hint of chocolate taste. "Nope. I never even saw it. Steve just told me that."

"Did you know Roberto Ramon?"

"Sure. He and Steve were friends. They went to Northeast High School together."

"Do you know anyone who might want to kill him?"

Isabel's eyes gleamed like glassy volcanic rock. "Wasn't that something? I couldn't believe it. I never knew anyone who was killed."

I'd known a few and each one had left me with a terrible taste in my mouth and a sick feeling inside. Sudden, violent endings are hard to accept. "Did he ever talk to you about being followed before he was killed?"

"Not to me. To Steve. Roberto would never talk to a woman about something like that. He was too proud. But he told Steve a man was standing outside his house. After that, he went out and bought a gun. I don't think he ever used it, but he had it just in case."

"Do you have any idea what he was doing at the Feinstein house the night Mrs. Feinstein was murdered?"

"Roberto was a hard worker and someone his customers could trust. If they needed him to work late, Steve would work late."

"He had a key to the house that was found in Mrs. Feinstein's bedroom."

"He did?" Her eyes went flat and hard. "He would never do anything wrong."

"I'm not saying he did."

Her face took on a look of recognition. "You think he was killed because he saw something at Mrs. Feinstein's house?"

"I don't know. Maybe."

"Wouldn't that be terrible? Poor Roberto. He was only doing his job. It just doesn't seem fair, does it?"

"No, it sure doesn't. Do you know Steve Ramirez?"

"No, I know a Johnny Ramirez. Who's Steve?"

"A friend of Roberto Ramon's. He lives in Tallahassee."

She shook her head and took out another chocolate. "No, I don't know any Steve Ramirez."

That real fuzzy feeling I have in the middle of a case when it's not going well was starting up in my stomach. I was happy to get out of the Sequendo's condo and head for my father's house. We were light years apart in political and religious values, but only two miles by my odometer.

CHAPTER FOURTEEN

My father lives in a two-story frame house set well back from the road. Its large porch sits empty and newly-painted. The front yard is deeply shaded by oaks and evergreens and covered by a Bahia-grass lawn.

Since his retirement, my father won't let anyone do any work around the house except him. He swears no one else can be trusted.

My father never answers the door on the first ring. He doesn't even answer on the fifth ring. I think he's getting a little deaf and I know he loves to control everything and everyone around him.

By the time his tall frame came lumbering toward the door, I was already sorting through his mail after having picked a few dead blooms off his miniature oleanders. "You gonna come in or what?" his deep voice boomed at me from his bearlike chest.

I turned and saw him standing on the steps, arms on his hips, sunlight streaking his crinkled gray hair and cutting his wrinkled face into even thicker folds than I remembered. He reminded me a bit of Archie Bunker in his blue work pants, white socks, black shoes and white shirt. I almost expected him to open his mouth and beller, "Edith!"

He looked as if he'd lost a little bit of the paunch he'd been carrying around. Without mom to cook him things he shouldn't have been eating anyway, the weight has slowly melted off him.

I gave him my best rebellious teenager voice and said, "Of course I'm coming in. I didn't drive all the way over here to do your yard work." It never ceased to amaze me how a visit with my father can reduce me to a simpering adolescent in ten seconds flat.

One of his big hands reached down and yanked letters out of my hands. "That's a federal offense young lady. The mail must go through, you know."

He was gruff, but behind that superficial nastiness pulsated a sweet man who probably wasn't aware of the power he held to make me feel guilty and angry in the same breath. He grunted at his mail. "Nothing but bills."

I shaded my eyes from the blazing sun. "I thought you were carrying on a correspondence with our state senators."

He thrust open the front door and surged inside, gently pushing me along. "I am," he grumbled, "but they don't answer me very often. I calculate the cost of postage is running three to one in my favor and still no change in the way those fools are doing business in Washington." My father is a confirmed conservative and chaunvinist who watched the Supreme Court confirmation hearings, staying solidly behind Thomas. I, of course, argued with him daily that Anita Hill couldn't be lying about being sexually harrassed because she had a reputation to lose. We almost came to blows over that one, but we squared off and settled for giving each other the silent treatment for a couple of days. Now he had summoned me to his house and I knew it had to have something to do with the Ted Sampson case.

I stepped into the foyer, admiring his new acquisition, a mahogany side table with satinwood inlay, or so he claimed. I'm not sure how he came by all these beautiful antiques. I know for certain it's not the way he said. Salvation Army and Goodwill do not have nineteenth century treasures for sale. Either he's lying to me about what he has or he's got some shady connections I'd rather not know about. Since I know next to nothing about antiques, only what I learn about on "Lovejoy," I didn't bother arguing with him.

He bounded toward his oak armchair, put his feet on the leather footstool and gave me a self-satisfied smile. "Lunch will be ready in a minute," he said. I could smell the scent of Italian bread crisping in the oven and the heady aroma of olive oil, garlic and peppers.

I took the peacock blue overstuffed chair across from him and looked out the French windows onto the stone terrace. Palms, silk floss trees and jacaranda measured off his yard. Around the room were a few more overstuffed chairs, a couch of flowery pastels, a huge wooden globe and built-in bookcases. His taste in reading ran to biographies and Second World War memorabilia. He'd been a sergeant in the Army and had seen most of Italy during his tour of duty.

Except for occasional forays into antique deals, he lived mostly in the past, remembering his days of glory in the police department and the Army. By comparison I suppose his present life seemed dull and almost pointless.

I've tried to interest him in a hobby or some volunteer work, but antiques and giving me a hard time are the only two things that bring a spark to his green eyes. He shuffled through the mail like a determined card hustler in some Los Vegas casino, then threw it in a laquered bowl. It had a feathery Japanese motif in red and black with gold trim. I have been coveting that vase for as long as I can remember.

He cleared his throat and I realized he was finally ready to get to me. "Steve Jefferson called me yesterday," he said.

"And what did he have to say?" I knew what the lieutenant had said, but my father and I play word games with each other. Code words for the deep feelings we have for each other, but have not brought ourselves to say.

"He's waiting to hear from you. Why haven't you checked in with him and how come when he calls you, you're never there?"

"I have a car phone, he can reach me," I said, more defensively than I'd intended. I vaguely remembered getting a message to call Lieutenant Jefferson, but quickly forgot about it. I really didn't have much to say to him other than that I didn't know anything.

My father's thick eyebrows knit together into a cross stitch. "You should call him. He's waiting."

I knew I could have given him another flip answer, but I also knew my dad was one of my best resources. He'd been a cop, a damn good one, and he knew his way around homicide cases. I took a deep breath and jumped in, "I'd call him, but I don't have one thing to tell him."

He shook his head disparagingly, causing me to feel the way I had in the fifth grade when I brought home a report card with one B on it. My father neglected the A's lined up in a row beneath and pounced on that one B. When I was ten, I think I fought off the tears. That afternoon I fought off the urge to run out of the room screaming. Instead, I cleared my throat. Then I told him about Ana Ramon, Dell Channing, Olivia Barton, Barry McCloud and Brenda Sampson.

He cocked an eyebrow at me, got up from his chair and motioned me to the kitchen. "You sure someone's not lying to you?" He opened the oven and took out a platter of stuffed peppers.

I shook my head and leaned against the counter, staring at the needlepoint sign my mother had made. *Don't Mess with the Cook* it read in perfect purple stitches.

I watched my father uncover a pot of tomato sauce and take a taste. At the risk of further humiliation, I said, "I really don't know what's happening on this one, Dad." I carefully avoided his eyes while I tried the sauce from the spoon he offered me.

He turned the burner on under a saucepan of water, then opened a cabinet and took out a package of linguini. "You aren't letting somebody bamboozle you, are you?"

I felt like defending every action I'd taken, but I forced myself to keep quiet and think about what he'd said. It felt like everybody had been deceiving me to some extent, but that's normal in a case as complicated as this one.

The one thing I wanted to keep secret from my dad was my attraction for my client. He'd really give it to me if he thought I was harboring lascivious feelings for Ted Sampson. Not that he hadn't probably run into the same thing when he was working, but for some reason that kind of thing was deemed okay for men. It was overlooked, just like the occasional crude or sexist remark they might make to the women working at the police station. It might not be the way it is today, but it was when he was in the thick of things.

My father poured some salt and oil in the saucepan of water, opened the package of pasta and turned on the heat under his sauce. He'd probably been cooking it for a day already and it had that dark red color only hours in a iron pot will produce. He turned and gave me a cryptic glance. "So what's your theory on this one?"

"I think my client has been framed, but I haven't been able to come up with any real evidence. It's all contradictory."

"Reminds me of the Boots Allen case," he said, dumping the linguine into the boiling water.

"The what case?"

"Boots Allen. It was before your time. Anyway, Boots Allen was supposed to have killed his mistress, Martha Thomas."

"Boots? Isn't that a little western for our neck of the woods?"

"They called him Boots because he always wore expensive alligator boots. Anyhow, it turned out there were at least three or four other people with enough motive to do her in. She wasn't a very nice lady."

"What happened?" I took down two plates from the cupboard and set them on the counter.

"Boots got off, but not until he was on death row and making his final appeal. They were already getting the acid ready for his chair when the dead woman's sister came forward. She claimed she'd known all along what happened, that she'd even been there the night her husband had killed Martha, but she'd kept silent. Once in a while she'd get drunk and blab to family or friends, but no one took it seriously."

I dangled a piece of linguine out of the pot and gave it the taste test. "How did you get on to the dead woman's sister?"

"A tipster." He took a loaf of garlic bread out of the oven and set it in a basket lined with a red cotton napkin.

"You think someone is going to come forward on this one with a confession?"

He dumped the cooked pasta into a colander in the sink. The steam rose around his head like fog. He jiggled the giant sieve around, then dumped the pasta back into its pot. "I don't know, Theresa, it's just a feeling I got." I helped myself to a plate of linguini, sauce, peppers and bread. Then I went over and sat down at the round maple table in the alcove behind the refrigerator.

My father's idea seemed a little weird to me, but I've known him to be right lots of times before. I began to wonder which of my suspects might come waltzing forward and help me solve the case.

CHAPTER FIFTEEN

The call from Dell Channing came in on my car phone as I was driving back from my father's house. I'd eaten too much, as I usually do when he cooks, and was feeling every minute of being forty. Maybe even seventy. I felt like I wanted a nap and a few hours of watching senseless sitcoms to bring back my brain from the regression a few hours with my father usually brings on.

Dell had located Laura Feinstein's script and wanted to know if I cared to see it. Do bats hang upside down in caves? Of course I wanted to see it. Besides, it detained me, at least for a little while, from encountering Aaron Feinstein.

Funny how the thought of meeting with an attractive man like Dell Channing can buoy me up. By the time I drove down Gulf Boulevard to his condo in Treasure Island, I was feeling about twenty-two again.

I pulled into the sixteen-unit building where Dell lived and inhaled a few breaths of Gulf air. Across the street from the Gulf of Mexico, a short driveway extended to a swimming pool by Boca Ciega Bay.

Cars were parked under their owner's units. A few years ago, insurers got tired of reimbursing Gulf Beach residents for water damage from winter storms and made it law that all buildings built from then on could not use the first floor for living space. Newer buildings can be easily spotted, rising up like dinosaurs on their cement blocks, fourteen feet above ground.

The beige stucco structure was new, only a couple of years old, but the surface was already cracking badly, showing signs of poor masonry or corrupt contracting. Corridors divided the building into four sections. Each opened into a courtyard of plants and sunlight. Green parrots shrieked at me from their nests atop tall palms while five lemon bottlebrush trees stood around a sign that read Treasure Island Lagoons.

A few tourists splashed each other in the small pool and an elderly man in red shorts and tee-shirt cast his line off the pier, probably hoping to catch a big one to brag to his friends up north about. I drove into a visitor slot beneath Dell Channing's building and took a look in the rear view mirror. After a windy drive over the causeway with my car windows open, my hair stood out in all directions. A few yanks of my brush through the tangles and a little lip gloss and I was ready to view Laura Feinstein's script.

My heart did anxious little pitty-pats as I hurried up the stairs to the third floor, refusing to share the elevator with an arrogant terrier who nipped at my shoe when I pushed the *up* button. His owner, an obese woman in a two-piece bathing suit, ignored her pet's aggressive action. Her face and arms were splotchy from sunburn so I suppose she was more worried about contracting skin cancer than a small lawsuit from a passing stranger.

I stopped outside unit 3D and rang the bell. The sound was like a blast from a foghorn. I suspected Dell Channing had purposely installed it to go with his nautical spirit. He opened the door and smiled.

His face was even tanner, more arrogant. He was in another tee-shirt, this time a bright yellow one with red letters, spelling out Yacht Basin in bold letters across the front. He wore faded blue jeans without a belt and his feet were bare.

Pleasure softened his eyes when he saw me. "Ms. Franco. Delighted," he said, making a sweeping gesture with his arm to welcome me inside.

I stepped into the air-conditioned room. To my right were the guest bathroom and a huge open almond and oak kitchen. The parquet floor held a few water spots, otherwise it gleamed back at me in the afternoon sun. Seascapes and oils of sailing ships decorated his walls. A boat in a bottle stood on his mantle above a huge stone fireplace, its three masts nearly touching the glass. "Glad you were free," he said, stepping over to the counter to pour a glass of chablis for himself and one for me.

I declined his offer. For some reason, I knew I had to keep my wits about me. He downed his wine and turned. "The script's in my storage bin below," he said, "I have the key right here." He patted the pocket of his shirt.

I followed Dell Channing out into the sunlit inner corridor. We turned and went down the stairway to ground level. He opened a heavy metal door, flipped on the light switch, and we stepped inside. A lone light bulb hung down from a water-damaged ceiling on an exposed cord. I wondered how Treasure Island Lagoons dared mock the fire marshall's code so blatantly.

The place smelled of packing boxes and mildewy luggage. Our shoes clacked across the cement surface past bicycles, gardening equipment and a pile of rafts for the swimming pool. I don't like tight, dimly lit places so I stayed only a step behind him. He took a sharp left turn into a maze of ceiling-to-floor lockers. Wooden bins with chicken wire around them stood in the center of the large room.

I felt the creepy feeling I've had just before something scary happens.

A man's voice shouted and a shot rang out, shattering the light bulb, bringing darkness and chaos with it.

One of us shrieked and I grabbed Dell's arm and shoved him out of the line of fire. He lost his balance, fell against me and knocked me down before he stumbled into one of the wooden bins. I heard the echo of footsteps and then a door slamming. I struggled to my feet and started for the door. Dell was right behind me, swearing loudly in my ear.

We raced to the door and ran outside. Someone had parked a bike in front of the entrance and we both tripped over it, sprawling to the cement. I muttered under my breath, feeling the pain sting across my knees and palms. I scrambled to my feet again and started to run.

I dodged from side-to-side, keeping low, hoping I wasn't a very good target, in case our attacker was still around. Heart pounding in my ears, I surged toward the street. A vehicle squealed out of the driveway and roared away before I could see it.

I leaned against a cement post, lungs shuddering for air, mouth dry, clothes drenched in sweat. I'd broken the heel off my flats and torn a hole in my slacks. Despite everything, I considered myself lucky. What I didn't like was that I'd let someone surprise us and that wasn't good.

Dell was standing on the edge of Gulf Boulevard, shaking a fist. His body trembled with rage or fear. I made my way to his side and grabbed for the neck of his tee-shirt. "Who else did you tell you had the manuscript?" He looked at me, his face a Rorschach of surprise and shock. "Who else?" I shouted, oblivious to the traffic pouring past us.

He gave me a haunted look. "No one." He took my hand and removed it from his shirt. "No one."

I didn't believe him. I turned and went back to my car to retrieve a flashlight before going into the storage room. It wasn't hard to discover which bin belonged to Dell. It had been broken open. The padlock dangled helplessly where someone had smashed the lathing. Torn cardboard boxes strew the floor, their contents spilling out on all sides.

I picked my way through the mess, wondering if I'd interrupted our attacker in time to save the script. I heard a sound behind me and whirled. In the shadows, a man stood staring at me and the jumble of belongings. My heart froze in icy fear. I raised the flashlight, ready to bonk him on the head if necessary.

"What the hell are you doing?" The voice was Dell Channing's. So was the body. I lowered the flashlight and took a deep breath. "I get real paranoid when I'm shot at and knocked down, so don't pull anything like that again."

"Sorry," he mumbled, looking penitent and holding out a new light bulb for the socket in a gesture of apology.

I nodded. "It's okay, I just didn't recognize you."

He smiled and the tension fled his face. "Have I changed that much in a few swift moments?" Before I could answer, he went to the socket and installed the new bulb. Dingy light descended on us and I turned off my flashlight.

He came over by the bin and surveyed the debris for a minute, then said, "I doubt they got anything of value."

I was still feeling a little shaken by being shot at, and angry at him that he hadn't thought enough of me and this case to at least retrieve the script before I got there. I snapped at him. "Maybe you didn't lose anything but the script."

"That didn't have any real value."

"Maybe not to you, but it must have had some value to someone. They broke in here to get it."

He shrugged. "I read it---skimmed it really---and I didn't see---"

"That's just it, you didn't see. Why did you leave it down here?"

"I don't have room for junk upstairs. You saw how small my condo is."

I suspected he was a narcissist who didn't have time for anyone or room for anything that didn't directly concern him. Now that Laura was dead, she was of little interest, and her belongings of less still.

"We should call the police," I said, hoping to get a rise out of him. Maybe he knew more than he was telling.

"I don't think so," he said. "What am I going to report? Some mildewed luggage, a useless script, a broken tennis racket?" He picked up the remains of some old 78s and tried to read their labels.

He looked too cocky for someone who had almost been shot. Besides, there was a touch of something in his face now that hadn't been there before. Maybe guilt.

He picked up a pile of papers and glanced at them. "Old IRS forms. I guess they weren't of much interest to the thief." He chuckled to himself and dropped the papers back into the bin. "One of these days I'll have to get this mess cleaned up."

"Do you think you could do me a favor and see if the screenplay is here?"

He smiled at me, then bent down and started to look. I relented a tad, realizing I'd been a bit hard on him. His space had been violated and that alone was enough to upset most people. My heart still hadn't settled back to its normal beat and my life had flashed before me in that second I heard the shot rip through the room and shatter the light bulb. That kind of jolting experience sometimes makes me wonder exactly what I was in this business for. All I saw was the muddle of other peoples' lives, rarely their good points. Was I like some psychic traveller, trying to help them sort through theirs in order to find meaning in my own? I knew I still hadn't found an answer to why my marriage had failed. Another woman was the quick answer, but a relationship doesn't fall apart because of a third person. The seeds of destruction have to be there for years, smoldering, ready to burst into full-scale cataclysm.

I hadn't resolved my mother's death either. I still had strong surges of guilt that I hadn't spent enough time with her when she was sick, the cancer draining her of her life energy in daily drips and dribbles. How many nights had I laid awake cursing myself for not taking better care of her, for not forcing her to take better care of herself?

I looked down at Dell Channing's broad back and saw his hands moving quickly, effortlessly, to pick up the pieces of his life. Although the idea he had been involved in the break-in had crossed my mind when I recognized him standing in the shadows a few minutes earlier, I had no proof he had anything to do with it. I shrugged, letting the annoyance I'd felt toward him evaporate. Maybe he was more upset by the break-in than he showed. If he was the macho guy I thought, he might not exhibit his hurt as recklessly as Brenda Sampson had.

I watched him dump some old ***Sailing*** magazines and the broken tennis racket into the trash can outside his bin. He salvaged a few Christmas ornaments but had to throw out most of the balls and lights. The fake Christmas tree was okay and so were the duffle bag and blue nylon carry-on luggage. His golf clubs and matching shoes looked no worse for the wear, but an old lamp was shattered and so were the wine goblets he'd left packed in a cardboard box.

He shuffled through a pile of papers, then looked up at me. "This is it." He handed me the manuscript and I clasped it to my breast as if it were a priceless relic. I left a little while later after he'd straightened up his bin and gone to call the condo manager to order a new lock installed. I'd been lucky the thief hadn't found the script, then again, maybe that wasn't what he'd been looking for.

CHAPTER SIXTEEN

I took Laura Feinstein's screenplay home with me, making only one quick stop at the 7-ll for some diet soda. I knew I drank too much of the stuff, but at least it was decaffeinated. Maybe all those preservatives and additives wouldn't eat away at my liver quite yet.

I locked my door, closed the blinds and lay back on the rattan settee in the Florida room. By mistake, or maybe on purpose, Dell Channing had included some of his personal letters and bills in the pile he handed me. The sea-faring gentleman had none of my compulsiveness. Or maybe his letters weren't as juicy as mine were.

I would never be so cavalier with my belongings. I kept any personal letters under lock and key. The diaries I had started in the eighth grade and continue to this day are safely locked away in a false-front cedar chest along with my divorce decree, two First Place medals I took in high school band competitions, and the Most Improved Player trophy I won at tennis camp years ago. I'd rather die than have someone I don't like read about my inner thoughts and find out my special secrets.

But that didn't stop me from reading Dell Channing's personal letters despite the pangs of guilt I felt. One was on peach note paper with a very strong scent of roses. The words were written in a tightly contained script with lavender ink. The envelope was addressed to him at his condo and carried the mark of some member of the insect world in the right hand corner. Trust Dell to treat love letters with exquisite care.

Darling Dell,

I'm writing you so you'll know how I really feel. I don't think I can stand being around Aaron much longer. He's such a prick! I really miss you and wish we could be together more often. Can't you swing it?

You're so much more of an adventurer and free thinker than I am. I wish I had the courage to do what you've done. If I did, I'd pack my bags and be out of here in an instant. But I'm a coward. Not a coward like Aaron is, but one nevertheless. I know you're always trying to tell me to be brave, but some of the things Aaron does nauseate me. He'd never hurt me, but I've seen humiliate friends and clients. The whole thing is pretty disgusting and I wonder why anyone puts up with it. As despicable as he is, he tolerates me, if not respect.

I yearn to get away, to cast fear to the wind and jump aboard your boat with you. Where is that island you want to sail to? I can just picture you with the sun shining down on your hair and your strong arms steering us to some grand adventure. The smell of salt air would be like ambrosia. I know I am becoming stronger and stronger and soon I will be able to break away from this dead marriage. Please be patient. We will have a lifetime together. Let me go at my own snail's pace, but know, above all else, that I do love you. Please don't give up on me.

Love forever,

Laura

I didn't know what to make of some of it. The letter certainly cast Mrs. Feinstein in a different light. From talking to people who had known her, I'd come to almost hate her. I thought I knew exactly why someone had killed her. After reading the letter, I wasn't sure. She seemed a vulnerable woman, afraid to leave her husband, yet yearning to break away.

I sipped on my soda and sat staring at the letter, holding it carefully as I read it again. I leaned back into the settee and stared up at the ceiling fan. It whirred and clicked, throwing a cool breeze down around me.

Something about the letter bothered me, but I wasn't sure what it was. It might have been that bit about Aaron Feinstein humiliating people and being a despicable person. If I read enough into that part, I might be able to conclude he was capable of killing his wife. But it took a lot of reading into it because Laura Feinstein also said her husband would never hurt her and that he treated her with respect.

I sighed and slumped down into the softness of the cushion. I was exhausted by frustration and the events of the week and probably wasn't thinking too well, but one other thing did hit me, foggy as I was. Laura Feinstein might not even have written the letter. I'd never seen her handwriting. Maybe Dell Channing wrote it and left it with the manuscript so I would find it. If so, why would he want me to read it?

I laid on the settee, skinned knees aching, hands still burning from the tumble I'd taken. My brain was hardly chock full of ideas, and the ones that were there didn't seem to lead anywhere. I forced myself to go back over the break-in at Dell Channing's condo earlier that day. Who had broken into Dell's storage area? It could have been someone Dell had paid to make it look as if he'd been burgled? But what would that do? It might have been a move to get my sympathy or throw suspicion onto someone else.

But if Dell hadn't staged it, then who had been the intruder? It could have been a man or a woman. Any of the people I'd spoken to over the past few days knew I was looking into Laura Feinstein's murder and might even have been tailing me. Someone had taken a shot at us. The bullet might have been meant for Dell or it might have been meant to just put out the light so the intruder wouldn't be recognized. The one possibility I shuddered to think about was that someone was after me.

I had no real proof the bullet was meant for me. But it could have been if I was getting close to something, something somebody didn't want to be discovered. A chill settled over my mind as I considered the idea. Then nausea crept up my throat and I tasted the burn of carbonation from too much soda.

I felt like going into my bedroom and crawling under the covers and not coming out for days, but my client expected more than that. Tired and confused as I was, I knew I'd never rest until I'd tied everything into a neat little package.

The obvious began to occur to me. Whoever killed Laura Feinstein had been safe while Ted Sampson was in prison. Now someone was in danger of exposure and my safety level was decreasing minute by minute.

The smell of barbecue came at me through the window and I realized I hadn't eaten for many hours, but I wasn't hungry. Fear does something to the digestive system.

Instead, I went into the bathroom and filled the tub. A nice lavender bubble bath was just what I needed to smooth away the aches and clear my head. I brought the screenplay with me, placing it on the floor where I could reach it once I was resting comfortably in the water.

I put my clothes in the hamper, remembered my promise to do a load of clothes and dumped everything into the washer along with a cup of soap. I shut the bathroom door on the thudding and wheezing noises emanating from my washing machine and stepped into the tub. I read in my bath when I can. Most days I settle for a shower because I don't have the time indulge in the luxury of a warm soak. When I do, I have it down to a science. I prop myself up against a soft towel, make sure there's enough water to cover me so I won't get chilled and stay submerged until I've finished my reading.

This time the water cooled before I finshed the manuscript. Dell Channing had been right, it was your typical sex/violence/fast-chase concept. Not one I particularily like, being partial to gooey romances, but the studios seemed to be making a lot more movies of the type exemplified by Laura's sceenplay than about adult relationships.

As far as I could see, there were no clues to Laura's death in the screenplay. The lead roles were played by two macho males. A woman did figure in a brief romantic triangle, but she exerted more power behind the scenes than directly. While I dried myself, I wondered if Laura was writing about herself. If she was, who were the two men? Her husband and Dell Channing? I couldn't discount Barry McCloud or even my client, Ted Sampson.

After reading it, I had no idea why anyone wanted to steal Laura's manuscript. On the other hand, I had no proof Laura had even written a script and if she had, whether this was it or not. Someone could have put her name on another person's script. That person was most likely Dell Channing, but I couldn't figure why he'd want to do such a thing.

I put some aloe vera on my knees and hands. It burned for a minute, then felt good. I wished I could get as quick a reaction on the cases I take. I still felt unsettled and frustrated. The bath hadn't done a thing for my peace of mind. I threw on some clean shorts and a long-sleeve shirt and headed for the beach. I walked halfway to the Don CeSar Resort, the pink princess that glorifies St. Petersburg Beach, before turning toward home. My barefeet had gotten a terrific workout on the shells and I was thinking of a short nap before going to see Aaron Feinstein.

I huffed into my driveway and nearly walked into Brenda Sampson's Miata. She was behind the wheel, resting her head on her hands. She didn't look good.

"Hello," I shouted, coming toward her side of the car.

Her head jerked up. She looked disoriented at first, then she said, "Your face is all red."

"I know. My face never sweats. It goes beet red." I leaned in her open window. "What can I do you for?"

Her face brightened and I was reminded of Jane Fonda in *Coming Home* when she sees John Voight for the first time. Brenda sniffed as if a tear or two might have entered her eyes. "I wanted to apologize for bending your ear the other night."

"No problem. You had a lot of things to get off your chest."

She smiled a genuine smile. "I never do that kind of thing. I hate women who do."

"Don't. Everybody needs somebody sometime." I was starting to sound like the lyrics of some western song I hate and so I said, "Want to come in for a drink?"

"Sure." She got out of the car, looking relieved that I'd asked her in. She was wearing a lime green jumpsuit of silky rayon and had pulled her thick brown hair into a knot on the top of her head. Her hair seemed to have a red tint to it, but maybe it was the light. She wore avocado-colored flats and carried a bright yellow bag on her shoulder. Small worry lines had gathered around her eyes and mouth and I wondered what she was upset about.

She followed me into my house. "I forgot to put the wash in the drier," I said over my shoulder. "Come along, it'll just take a minute."

She nodded and followed behind me like a girl scout on a tracking expedition. She paused to study the photos of my mom and dad I'd put on the shelves of a rattan etagere. "Your parents?" she called to me from the living room.

"Yup. Typical, but nice." I dumped the wash into the dryer, turned it on and went back into the living room. She was sitting on the rattan settee, flipping through a book on organic gardening. She looked up and smiled. "Mine still think I'm fourteen years old. My mother told me that the other day. Do you believe it?"

I nodded and went into the kitchen. She padded behind. I offered her some cranapple juice and she accepted. We stood, sipping our juice and trying to avoid each other's eyes. Finally I said, "Let's go sit in the Florida room. Much cozier."

We walked past the étagère and I wondered if she'd opened any of the drawers while I was with the wash. Paranoia moves in on me when anyone connected with a case comes to my house, making me wonder what Brenda really wanted.

I sat on the edge of a white wicker chair and glanced at my watch. "You must have left aerobics early."

"I have a late class so I conned one of the instructors into filling in for me until then."

"Why?"

"You don't believe I simply want to apologize?"

"I suppose I could, but my gut feeling says, no."

"Do your gut feelings ever lie?" She took a sip of her juice and gave me what might have been a wink.

It threw me. I'd been winked at by men, but never by a woman. I wasn't sure if she was asking me to join her in a secret or if she was coming on to me. Whichever, I felt uncomfortable, the kind of discomfort that makes me reach up with one of my feet and plant it squarely in my mouth. My mouth blurted out words before my mind had time to censor them: "You didn't kill Laura Feinstein did you?"

She flushed, but it could have been at my directness. "Of course not." She laid her head back and hooted. When she'd stopped laughing, she sat forward and said, "You think I came here to confess or something like that?"

I set my glass down on the small table beside me. "Stranger things have happened."

She shook her head wearily. "No, you've got it all wrong. I thought we'd made a connection the other night and I wanted to see if it was real." She shook her head again, set down her glass and stood. "I guess I'd had a little too much rum. Sorry for the intrusion."

"Wait," I stood up and took hold of her wrist. It was cool and dry, like a snakeskin. Last night I had felt a sisterly connection with the Brenda and I hoped the reptilian sensation was one like the green snake that brings life energy and not the black snake of deception.

For some reason since I'd met her ex-husband, I was constantly unsure of my reactions to people. I didn't know whether it was fair to blame it on Ted Sampson, but I was doing it anyway.

She turned and looked at me with hurt in her eyes. I sighed and gave her my best hopeless gesture. "I'm sorry again. Big foot in big mouth is my only excuse."

The space between her brows wrinkled, then flattened out as her face started into a smile. I felt a reaction of pure relief and affection for the woman. "All right," she said, tossing her hair back from her face with her hand. "I accept."

We walked back to the Florida room and sat down again. She turned toward me with a look of complete sincerity. "If Ted didn't kill Laura, I'm as interested as you are in finding out who did. I need some justification for having married the big lug. Even it's only that he didn't murder Laura Feinstein."

Although the words didn't make exact sense, coupled with her facial expression, they were compelling. "The truth is always better than not knowing." Why I start mumbling cliches during emotional moments, I'm not sure. My psychiatric nurse friend, Sarah, once told me it might be because I'm uncomfortable with feelings. Some day I'm going to have punch out that woman for always being right.

Brenda fingered the side of her temple. "You don't believe he's really innocent, do you?"

"Most of the time I do."

"Except when he lies to you."

"Except when he lies to me." We both giggled and the tension in the room evaporated.

"Are you getting anywhere with the case?"

I shrugged. "I really can't tell you too much. Client privilege and all that stuff. But if you have any more information that might help, shoot it to me. Maybe it will bring this thing to a close sooner."

"I really haven't come up with anything more, but you'll be the first to know."

"I wish somebody would let me know something."

"It's not going well then?"

"Nope. I don't have a real feel for what's going on. A lot of people are lying, but that's normal in a case like this."

"But it doesn't help, does it?"

Either Brenda had learned some pretty useful psychiatric skills or she was listening and empathizing with everything I was saying. That felt pretty good after days of people playing games with me. I gave her a grateful smile. "I think we connected the other night, too. It was the first time in a long time I let someone know my real feelings."

"It's probably hard in your line of work not to wear a mask."

"How true that is."

"You ought to go easier on yourself. You haven't been at this case that long, have you?"

"Seems like forever, but it's only a few days."

Brenda wrinkled her nose. "I've been wracking my brains for answers. Maybe Olivia Barton did kill Laura."

"What makes you say that?"

"I was thinking about that day I told you about, when Laura slapped Olivia."

"And?"

"I remembered something else Olivia had said. It was another day, before that. She was talking about getting a gun to protect herself. I told her she'd probably end up shooting herself in the foot or something like that. I'd just read an article about how people who buy guns to protect themselves either are terrified at the moment of truth when an intruder faces them or they shoot themselves or a loved one by mistake."

"What did Oliva say?"

"She laughed. But the color drained out of her face and there was something really wicked in her eyes. I hadn't seen it before."

The atmosphere in the room had gone chill. It reminded me of when I was a teenager and we used to tell ghost stories late at night at slumber parties and scare ourselves half to death. My voice came out shaky and adolescent. "Then what happened?"

"Olivia told me she'd once been arrested in a murder case but had been released."

I scanned through my brain computer banks. Nothing like that had turned up in my earlier check of Olivia Barton's life. Florida is funny that way, though. People can get their files sealed endless times if they know the right judge or know how to play the courtroom game. Olivia hadn't struck me as being particularily savvy, but she might be an entirely different person in the legal arena.

"Did she mention any of the details?"

"No, and to tell you the truth, I didn't want to hear any. The idea of murder gives me the creeps."

A chill ran up my legs as I thought about Olivia Barton. If she was capable of murderous intent, as most of us are, was it strong enough for her to kill Roberto Ramon and Laura Feinstein? It was something worth checking into. I read somewhere that murder gets easier each time. I didn't want to think that such a beautiful woman could be a murderer, but I knew they came in all shapes and sizes.

Brenda left a little while later and I called my Dad to see if he remembered an arrest for Olivia Barton. He didn't, but said he'd check with his cronies. While I folded my laundry I thought about Olivia. There were a few judges who could be bought or coerced. Olivia was beautiful enough to hold sex or some other favor above a lonely judge's head in exchange for silence. I hated to be reminded of how the system worked, but a little dose of reality never hurts.

CHAPTER SEVENTEEN

I had some weird dreams that night. Sarah, my psychiatric nurse friend is a student of Jungian dream analysis. She once gave me a quick course in unlocking my dreams. She told me people who are in direct communication with their inner selves use dreams less often to get attention for their needs, but the rest of us are getting constant jolts from the unconscious as it tries to set up a dialogue.

"Everything in your dream is an aspect of you," she said. "And only you can decipher the meaning of your dreams. They have meaning within the context of your life." Despite what Sarah had said, I wasn't sure I wanted to decipher the dreams I had that night. The only complete dream I remembered when I woke up was of a glacier. It was a huge monolith of ice and cold. I was tempted to move closer to the glacier, but I was afraid. The glacier started melting and behind it, I saw an old pirate ship with rotten, tattered sails hanging from its masts. Pirates ran around in a frenzy, repairing it, shouting and pushing one another. Something drew me closer and I climbed up a ladder that led right to the deck. I was awed by what I saw, sensing something important was happening on the ship.

A grizzled old man in a red bandana and gold earring grabbed me by the wrist and brought me to a table laden with wine and cheese. He winked at me and said, "If they find out what's in the hold, we're in for it." We laughed about that, although I wasn't sure what was so funny.

After we'd eaten, he opened the hatch to show me what was below. I peered down into the darkness. The stench was awful and I could hear moaning and the clanking of chains. I tried to get away, but he laughed and pushed me down a ladder. Prisoners were shackled to the walls and I went around releasing them as quickly as I could. Dell Channing was there, so were Olivia Barton, Ted Sampson and Brenda. Even my mother was there. She was thin and hungry, but when I tried to feed her, she wandered away.

I woke up drenched in sweat. My body ached, full of fatigue and haunting memories. I dragged myself out of bed and made some tea. Then I sat on the settee, trying to figure out my dream. If my suspects weren't going to tell me what was going on, maybe my dream would. When I closed my eyes and tried to return to that pirate ship, I realized the pirate was that part of me that feels I can have whatever I want without asking. That was the part that had accused Brenda. It wasn't a part of me I used often nor one I was proud of, but it was there just the same.

The best I could do with the hold was to assume it was the hidden part of me I'm afraid to bring out into the open in the clear light of day and examine.

Sarah told me you can talk to your dream fragments in the daylight and have a dialogue with them, but I wasn't sure this could happen and even if it could, I wasn't ready to do that yet. My mother had looked so terrible in the dream, I was afraid what she might say if I did talk to her.

The figures of Dell Channing, Brenda and Ted Sampson and Olivia Barton remained blurry and unformed. I still had no idea what they were doing in my dream, but I had faith that their meaning would come to me. When it did, I felt I would know more about who killed Laura Feinstein. I knew that didn't make logical sense, but then dreams are not rational creations.

Before I had a chance at a second cup of tea, my phone rang. It was Ana Ramon. She told me her mother-in-law was back home with her and was doing well. She said her only regret was that Angel's mother hadn't found anyone dependable to babysit for the little girl.

"Glad to hear about Mrs. Ramon," I said, still feeling a little shaky after my dream.

"She's a tough old lady. She'll come through." She paused and we both had our thoughts about tough old ladies. "I called you because I heard from Jerry Ramirez."

"Jerry Ramirez?"

"The guy Roberto went to stay with when he was afraid someone was chasing him."

"Oh, that Jerry Ramirez. What did he say?" I played with the phone cord and hoped it was good news.

"He's in Vero Beach, on vacation I guess, planning to take the kids to the space center and Disneyworld. He said he'd talk to you about Roberto if you wanted to make the trip."

"I can't phone?"

"Nope. He sounded real tight, like he picked up some of Roberto's fear from someplace."

"Guess I'd better make the trip then." I got the details of where to find Jerry and hung up. I hate long drives, but if talking to Jerry Ramirez would blow open the case, so be it.

I made an omelette with plenty of vegetables and cheese to fortify myself. I'd take some snacks and maybe a sandwich or two. When I passed by the bathroom mirror, I took a quick look at my face. I put on an oatmeal and honey scrub before I climbed into the shower. I figured I might meet some nice guy on the trip and I could use a little glow to my complexion.

I put on my best pair of jeans and a good rayon shirt that doesn't show wrinkles or dirt. Inside a small bag, I stowed some underwear, a nightshirt, a pair of socks and my toothbrush, in case I had to stay overnight. It was a long drive to the Atlantic coast and I didn't know what might happen after I talked to Jerry Ramirez.

Before I left, I called Mike and told him I thought Joe Latimore was trying to pull a fast one. My ex-husband chuckled and told me good-naturedly that if I didn't come up with something soon, they were probably going to settle.

"Settle? The guy is walking around with very little difficulty, driving at breakneck speeds, and probably even had the nerve to climb up and patch the hole in his roof. If he's injured, I'm Queen Elizabeth!"

"Don't take this personally, Terry," he said, probably putting his size ll's up on his desk, loving every minute of our conversation. He likes to see me sputter and fume about principles and fair play. "There are things about this case that make it look like a settlement is the only way."

"Don't you guys ever worry about being cheated?"

"Not too much."

I made some kind of animal noise of disgust, knowing my insurance premium would probably go up to pay for Joe Latimore's case. That really burned me and so I said, "Don't settle until the end of week. I promise to have proof positive by then."

"You in the miracle-working business?" he said. I could just picture the smug look on his self-righteous face.

"No miracles. Just promise me."

"Okay, okay. 'Til the end of the week."

"And don't bug me about it."

"Do I ever?"

"Sometimes." I hung up before I revealed I was going out of town. If he knew I was doing that, he'd probably take back our agreement. He was just the kind of black snake to do it, too.

I slipped a note under Evelyn's door telling her not to worry if she didn't see me for a day or two. I wasn't sure she'd call my dad if I didn't show up, but I didn't need him hounding me on my return in case things got sticky in Vero Beach.

I wasn't relishing the monotonous ride to the other coast, but it was the only way to find out what Jerry Ramirez knew. Highway 60 is a two-lane road that begins east of Tampa and goes nearly straight across to Vero Beach. At first it's a pleasure to drive along it after the rough and tumble of the Howard Franklin Bridge, with its gaggle of trucks weaving in and out of traffic on that huge expanse over Tampa Bay, pushing 65 m.p.h., trying to force the slower drivers out of the way. Then follows the even more hectic pace of cars zooming onto 275 North, cutting me off after a driver or two realizes he nearly missed the turn-off for Highway 4 to Orlando.

After that, Highway 60 seems like a tranquil stretch of trees and foliage. It passes a few small towns like Mulberry and Alturas, but mostly heads through a greener part of Florida. Cows laze in pastures and pine trees loom up alongside the road. It's a flat stretch, the kind that can hypnotize you after a while into nearly driving off the road. That's when I take out my Harry Connick, Jr. tapes and pretend I am in tap dancing class to keep from going stir crazy.

I made only one pit stop in Lake Wales and pulled in Vero Beach about two o'clock. It was one of those picture postcard days with the Atlantic surf coming in white and foamy and the ocean a perfect blue-green. I stopped at a gas station, relieved myself, combed my hair, and finished off half a sandwich and a few slugs of water from my thermos.

I arrived at the Palms Motel, the place Ana Ramon said Jerry Ramirez was staying, about two-twenty. If there were any palms in the area, I didn't see them. A two-story brick structure badly in need of a new roof stood next to a bedraggled pine forest. The swimming pool was padlocked and surrounded by a high chain link fence. A sign told me to Keep Out. Friendly place.

Inside the motel, a painfully thin man with a lit cigarette clenched between his teeth looked out from behind a soiled red curtain when the bell announced my entrance. His badge said Bruce. I was betting he also lived nearby when he pushed a very big and curious boxer back behind a curtain behind him. He said between clenched teeth: "Stay, Henry, this lady don't want you sniffing up her crotch."

I was impressed by Bruce's intention if not his word choice. His face was long and narrow, surrounded at the chin by a tuft of shaggy beard. He was nearly bald, but combed what little hair he had across the oily expanse of his head, probably thinking no one would notice. His color was a washed-out white, as if he never ventured outside into the sunshine. He wore a faded red tee-shirt and a black polyester vest above his shiny black pants. Scuffed cowboy boots completed his ensemble.

His eyes were green. They reminded me of bottle glass, the kind Heineken comes in, but I doubted the man drank anything pricier than Muscatel. He looked like the kind of person who might spit on the floor, so I kept my distance.

I took out my friendly visitor voice and said, "What's going on with the pool?" He talked through the cigarette in his teeth. "Nothing serious. Time to add chlorine. You wouldn't want to fry your skin off, now would you?"

At that moment, he reminded me a little of Norman Bates, so I cut to the important talk. "Can you ring Jerry Ramirez and tell him I'm here to see him?"

He lifted an eyebrow and gave me the once over. I felt like he'd half-undressed me, so I folded my arms across my chest and leaned against the counter, just in case he had x-ray vision. His eyes glazed over for a second, then he blinked and said, "He ain't here. Went to Disneyworld with the family. Glad he took those two squawking kids out of here. They were disturbing Henry." He looked back toward the curtain. The black muzzle of the dog was poking through between the two soiled curtains as if he wanted to participate in the conversation. "Henry's a very sensitive pooch, ain't ya, Henry?"

The dog squealed and the curtain wafted back and forth as if some mysterious force, or a dog's tail, were moving it. Bruce stared at it, smiling with a look on his face that told me that moving curtain might turn out to be his afternoon's entertainment.

I tapped on the counter to get his attention. "When is he expected back?"

Bruce sniffed and wiped his nose with the back of his hand. "He don't tell me about his plans."

"I suppose not. Here's my card. Would you ask him to call me when he gets back?"

Bruce took the card and set it on the counter next to a vase of plastic flowers. "I'll tell him, but I can't guarantee he'll call."

I nodded. "That's okay, I'll check back with you later." I headed for the door and drove the short distance to the beach. Once there, I took off my shoes, rolled up my pant legs and shirt sleeves and took a long walk across the sand.

A brisk breeze had come up and a few kids ran along by the water, lifting their kites into the air. Their homemade toys rose skyward, shiny papers of silver, blue and yellow, cutting across the broad expanse in airborn delight. I waved to one little boy and he waved back, his freckled face glowing in the afternooon sun. I headed south, strolling along the edge of the water, sometimes stopping to pick up a shell or dip my feet into the cool water.

Time slipped away and before I knew it, the sun was moving close to the horizon. I dried my feet, put my shoes back on and crawled into my car. My lips tasted of salt and sun, and I felt relaxed and hungry. I almost talked myself into believing I was on vacation, not tracking information on a murder case.

When I arrived back at the Palms Motel, Bruce informed me Jerry Ramirez hadn't come back yet. Although I didn't want to spend the night, it was looking more and more as if I was going to have to. I gave Bruce my credit card and after he ruined two or three forms, he finally gave me an imprinted one to sign. He handed me a key to room 3A. "That's up on the second floor, next to the soda machine."

Although there were no cars in the parking lot, he acted as if he was doing me a big favor to swap my key for a corner room. "Most folks like the convenience of ice and soda," he said, indicating by his tone of voice there was something wrong with my moral fiber.

I got my little bag and some reading material out of my car, then I headed up the stairs to my room. It was a dreary place with a sagging double bed and threadbare wall-to-wall carpeting in a pea green. A chair that looked like the inside of a teflon pot stood in the corner next to a plastic palm. At least I'd discovered whence came the name for the Motel. A brass lamp in need of polishing stood on a small desk in the corner next to a Gideon Bible.

I almost went downstairs and checked back out, but I didn't want to miss Jerry Ramirez and there wasn't another motel nearby, so I stayed. I dropped my belongings on the yellow bedspread, wondering how long it had been since it had seen the inside of a washing machine. The bathroom was tiny, with only a small shower. The toilet ran softly and continually and I made a mental note to report that fact to Bruce in case he had any interest in fixing it.

I hung my clothes on a hook behind the door and took a long shower. Already I regretted not bringing more to wear. I dried myself with a stiff pink towel that reminded me of the kind my grandmother used for rags. I put on clean underwear and socks and pulled on my pants and shirt. After combing my hair and applying lip gloss, I lay down on the bed and read through the restaurant section in the yellow pages. I called for a pizza and then only ate half of it. Feeling stuffed and bloated, I tried to read a beach newspaper I'd picked up outside my door, but found my mind kept going back to Ana Ramon's call.

If Jerry Ramirez wanted to see me, why wasn't he there? Had he become the next victim in the chain of deaths that seemed to follow after Laura Feinstein's murder? It gave me goosebumps to contemplate it. I was spooked enough in St. Petersburg where I knew the players and the turf. Here I was unfamiliar with people and places and could be a sitting target for anyone who cared to eliminate me, if I was getting too close to the truth.

I called Ana's number, but got no answer. Just as well I supposed, because she probably couldn't tell me anything I didn't already know. I dozed off a couple of hours later, sometime between *MacGyver* and *Night of The Living Dead.*

A knock on my door awoke me and I stumbled toward the door. My internal time clock told me it was sometime after midnight, but exactly how much past I didn't know. The knock came again, this time more urgent and I picked up the Gideon Bible in case I needed to bean whoever was on the other side of the door. "Ms. Franco?" said a deep male voice.

"Yes?"

"It's Jerry Ramirez. I have to talk to you."

"I'll meet you in the lobby in five minutes," I said, figuring it was not a good time to invite strange men into my bedroom. Footsteps clicked away from the door and I went into the bathroom and splashed water on my face. I also washed off the tomato sauce that must have lodged on my cheek during my battle with the pizza.

When I arrived in the motel lobby, Bruce was standing behind the counter in his bathrobe, a red velour monstrosity with mustard stains down the front. What little hair he had was standing up at the sides of his head, and for a moment he reminded me of one of the Three Stooges --- Mo, I think. Henry yipped from behind the curtain until Bruce gave a whistle and the dog retreated into quiet.

Jerry Ramirez was a man of medium-height with deep brown eyes that weren't exactly sinister, but held something that made me feel uneasy. Except for the thin black moustache above his upper lip, he was cleanshaven. He smiled at me with the kind of smile someone gives when they are about to lie to you. He was deeply tanned, the way a person was who either worked in the sun all day or spent his time on the beach.

I glanced at the clock hanging on the wall and saw it was three a.m. Jerry Ramirez looked fresh and awake as if he was used to staying up late and enjoying it.

"Ms. Franco. I'm so glad you came."

I shook the hand he offered, thankful that Bruce was watching over us. "I heard you wanted to talk to me," I said, hoping I looked better than I felt.

"That's right," he said, heading for a burnt orange couch with a tear in the left arm rest and stepping just out of earshot of the owner. Jerry motioned me to sit. I sat.

His voice was high-pitched, tense. "It's about Ramon. Ana told me you were trying to find out who killed him."

"That's right. What do you know about his death?"

"I know he was spooked, man." The light from a cheap fixture on the ceiling splattered across his face, revealing a nearly invisible scar from his left cheek to his jawline. I wondered if he'd been in a fight, but decided not to ask. Jerry continued talking in a slow, deliberate tone, as if he was measuring his words carefully. "Roberto called me half a dozen times from St. Pete. At first I thought he was drinking tequila again."

"He used to drink that stuff?"

He nodded and gave me a disgusted look. "When he lived in New Mexico. He brought me a bottle once and I refused to drink it. It had a worm or something in it."

I remembered one New Year's Eve when I was in high school and somebody tried to get me to drink some from the bottle. I had the exact same reaction.

Jerry Ramirez scowled. "Whatever it was, it shouldn't have been in that bottle, man."

At least we shared a distaste of tequila. Whatever else we shared was yet to be discovered. I turned toward Jerry and said, "Tell me what happened before Roberto died."

"He called me. He sounded desperate. Anyhow, I couldn't make out all the story. I only knew he was scared. More than I'd ever known him to be and we'd been in some pretty weird situations, me and Roberto."

"What was he scared of?"

"He was sure somebody was after him."

"Did he say who?"

"No. I don't think he knew."

"I understand he came up to stay with you."

"Yeah. I told him, 'Come here, man, it's safe up here.'" He scowled again. "Maybe I shouldn't have told him."

"You found him, right?"

"That's right. I'd been out working and I came home. My wife and the kids were at her mother's. There was poor Roberto, lying on the floor, his head bashed in. I've seen a lot of things, but none of them were worse than that. The rug still has a blood spot on it. My wife never could get it out and she's a whiz at stuff like that." He shook his head. "It was a damn shame. Roberto was a good friend. A good man."

His words took me back to Roberto's mother's house. She had said basically the same thing. It's one thing when a scoundrel gets it, but when a man who is loved dies, it's a hundred times worse. Let them all die in their beds of old age after having lived a good life, I say. But then, I'm not in charge of those things. Everything he'd told me, except the part about the bloodstain on the rug, I already knew. I looked at the man and tried to figure out what additional information he had to add to my notes. Not being very psychic, I did the next best thing. I asked him. "So what did you want to tell me?"

"Tell you?" He gave me a look of surprise and fear.

"You told Ana you wanted to see me."

Ramirez's face closed over as if a screen had come down, shadowing any emotion from my eyes. He nodded. "Sure. I told her I'd talk to you and I have."

"But she said you didn't want to talk to me on the phone."

"That's right." His eyes flickered, then held in a vague stared. "Who knows who might be listening in."

"But you haven't told me anything I didn't already know."

He stood up and did a little half-bow that in no way made up for the disappointment I felt. I don't take kindly to long drives and runarounds. I stood up beside him, coming nearly to his chin. I probably sputtered a bit when I said, "What is this, some kind of game?"

He shook his head and backed toward the door. "No game, honest. I told you everything I know." He exchanged a male eye gesture with Bruce and smiled at me before he said, "I got to get back to my wife now or she'll think I'm out with some other woman." He paused at the door and snickered. "Then again, I have been."

I listened to the sound of his laughter echoing down the hall. Bruce chuckled to himself. "Nice guy. Friend of yours?"

I didn't bother to answer the manager, I just turned on my heel and headed for my room and a few hours of agitated sleep. Someone or something had scared Jerry Ramirez after he spoke to Ana. I knew I'd probably never find out who or what it was. One thing was for sure: Jerry Ramirez wasn't going to tell me. I almost went and knocked on his door and routed his wife out of bed, but I knew that wouldn't do any good. When someone is running scared, they won't talk to me. If I used stronger methods, maybe. But as it was, I had to settle for whatever people wanted to share with me. Sometimes that was precious little.

CHAPTER EIGHTEEN

I had a hard time falling asleep after my encounter with Jerry Ramirez. When I finally dropped off, I couldn't wake myself up, even after the couple in the next room had a big fight and started bouncing furniture off the walls.

Maybe my drowsiness was because it was a foggy morning and I'd have loved to stay under the covers. It might also have been lack of sleep or the feeling of depression that had settled over me when I discovered Jerry Ramirez had pulled a fast one on me and there was nothing I could do about it.

About 8:30 a.m., I finally dragged myself off the bed. I took another shower, this time with cold water. The other residents must have been early risers as well as clean people because there wasn't a drop of warm water available. I dried my shivering body, then glanced at my reflection in the mirror as I passed by. Deep circles cut under my eyes and my face had a sallow color. I splashed cold water on my face from the sink and settled for some makeup under my eyes and some blush on my cheeks. My clothes smelled of Bruce's cigarette smoke, perspiration and a sweet smell I thought must be room deodorizer. I didn't want to pull on those pants and shirt again, but I had no choice.

When I got down to the front desk, Bruce was behind the counter with a smile on his face. A lit cigarette smoked beside him on the counter in a Disneyworld ashtray. He looked as if he'd just won the lottery or at least had slept a few more hours than I had.

He wore the same black polyester vest and pants, but he'd traded the faded red tee-shirt for a white one with the words, *Life is a Beach*, emblazoned in Dayglow orange across it. When he stepped out from behind the counter to hand me a morning paper, I noticed his feet sported a pair of scuffed sneakers instead of the cowboy boots he'd worn the day before. Very nice, Bruce, perhaps you'll make the best dressed list this year. Lack of sleep makes me a catty person.

Henry, the sniffing dog, was not around. Perhaps he was out chasing squirrels or smelling female passers-by. "Care for a continental breakfast?" asked Bruce breezily.

"No, thanks," I said, feeling the need for something more substantial than watered down orange juice and a stale roll.

His face was eager. "Comes with the room."

"Nah, I'm on my way out."

He took a deep drag on his cigarette and I felt a wave of nausea wash over me. Since I quit smoking, I can't bear the smell of someone else's smoke.

I checked out and then found a little diner where I filled up on scrambled eggs, hash browns, bran muffins and half a grapefruit. I washed everything down with three cups of tea. By then I started to feel human.

I filled my car up with gas and headed out of town. Sunlight was beginning to slice through the clouds, leaving the land shimmering in lavenders and greens. The drive back to St. Petersburg was uneventful except for an accident on the highway that drew four State troopers and a bunch of gawkers. I'm not sure what excites people about the sight of fellow human beings in distress, but something does. Maybe they're just trying to re-affirm that they're alive and well and the victims aren't. Or maybe they're just bloodthirsty.

When I pulled into the driveway, I saw my landlady pruning her oleanders A pair of white tights clung to her tall legs and a magenta overblouse with a round collar came down almost to her knees. A white bandana was tied around Evelyn's head, making her bright red hair stand out dramatically from her face. White earrings swung from her lobes and her sneakered feet were nearly buried in the seaweed she'd placed around her plants.

"It's the best fertilizer around and costs nothing," she'd told me countless times. "I wish people would wake up and realize those artificial fertilizers are expensive, don't work half the time, and end up polluting our water."

Evelyn was right about that. She was an environmentalist long before it was fashionable to be one. She came over to my car and poked her tanned face in my window. Her deep brown eyes carried the usual amount of intelligent energy. The woman never seemed to tire.

"Where have you been?" she chimed, running a glove over my car. "Looks as if this little beauty could use a wash."

I hate washing my car and usually pray for rain so I won't have to bother with it. I smiled back at Evelyn. "I've been to the market to buy a fat hog."

Evelyn stepped back and opened the door for me. "Home again, home again, jiggety jog." She peered in the back seat as if I might have a stranger tied back there against his will, then she whirled and pulled me out of my seat. Her arm came around me as we walked and she giggled softly into my ear. "Benjie asked me to go with him to his niece's wedding next Saturday. Can you believe it?"

"Of course. He adores you. You're going, I hope."

Her face looked young, girlish, at that moment. "I don't know. I don't really want to encourage him."

"Why not?"

"At my age? What would people say?"

"What do you care?"

She giggled again and gave me a squeeze. "You're right, you know. What do I care?"

After I'd gone inside, I saw her out in her garden, singing. Young love is great, but mature love is even better. Sometimes I think I'll never experience it myself, but who knows? My mind quickly flitted to Ted Sampson and I wondered why I kept thinking about him in a romantic way.

While I took off my clothes and pulled on a robe, I remembered my encounter with Jerry Ramirez and all the people I'd talked to the last few days. I wasn't sure whether I should tell Ted about how little progress I had made or not. I kept hoping something would break, but so far, everything had turned out to be a false lead. I decided to have a cup of tea and then soak in a hot bath. Before I could finish my drink, a BMW pulled up in the driveway and my heart did a little flipflop. Ted Sampson sat behind the wheel, a big smile on his face. Evelyn stared at him, then waved to me before she ducked behind an oleander.

Ted got out of his car and walked toward my door. By then, my heart was pounding so loudly I couldn't even hear his shoes clicking up the cement. I looked down at the spaghetti sauce stains on my mint green chenille robe. I felt grubby and unprepared. I waved at him through my kitchen window and tried to straighten my hair before I rushed to the door.

"Sorry to bother," he said through the screen door, a smile moving across his splendid features.

"You're not bothering, it's only that I just got back from the other coast and--"

"You've been to California?"

"No, to Vero Beach."

We both laughed and I jiggled the lock nervously until it sprang open.

"Come on in," I said, trying to usher him past the kitchen and into the living room. I felt a little silly in my bathrobe, but he seemed perfectly at ease. As usual. I wondered if anyone or anything rattled him.

He stopped in the kitchen entryway and grabbed an apple from a fruit bowl. His nonchalance annoyed me and I said rather crossly, "You caught me at a bad time."

"Shall I come back later?" he said, taking a step backward. He gave me one of his endearing smiles and my anger melted away.

Suddenly I was terrified that if he left, he might not ever come back, so I said, "No, no. Come on in and sit down."

He sat on the rattan settee by my desk and smiled at me. "I thought maybe we could catch an early supper and you could fill me in on what's happening with my case."

I wanted to tell him how I needed a few more hours sleep and a long soak in the bath tub, and that we could meet for breakfast the next day. But instead I found myself saying, "Sure, an early dinner sounds great." I felt his eyes on me as I started for the bathroom. I turned at the door and drew the collar of my robe more tightly around me.

"Just let me catch a quick shower and I'll be right with you."

I rushed into the bathroom, dropping my robe on the floor. The shampoo and strawberry soap washed away the grit from my long trip. My worries about Jerry Ramirez spun down the drain along with the residue of an expensive shampoo and creme rinse I reserved for special occasions. If going out for dinner with Ted Sampson wasn't a special occasion, I didn't know what was.

We drove to Gulf Boulevard and headed south toward the pearl of the beaches, an old lady of class among the glitzier resorts. Transplendent in Don CeSar pink, she stood on the edge of Pass-A-Grille, lit from above by the stars and from below by discreet spotlights.

I had worn my green silk dress, but I wasn't sure even that was elegant enough for the King Charles room. I'd heard about the harpist and the expensive prices and wondered if I'd feel as uncomfortable as I usually did when waiters flitted around the table, catering to our every need.

"Have you been here before?" Ted asked, once we'd settled into the plush banquette overlooking the Gulf of Mexico. The harpist was playing a jazzy piece softly, inobtrusively. I stared at her flowing gown. "No, I've never been here. Have you?"

"Not for a long time." His blue eyes went slightly grey, as if he were remembering a particularly dismal period in his life. While he studied his menu, I studied him. His jawline was strong and well-crafted, with a cleft in his chin I yearned to reach out and touch.

He read the entrees aloud to himself and I mused about his perfect white teeth. He smiled at one point and the skin around his blue eyes crinkled. His brows were thick and just a tad unruly. He had small hands, small bones in his wrists and a feathering of brown hair at the cuff. Although he didn't look me in the eyes, there was something else about him, smoldering and obscure, a sense of sexuality that surfaced when he turned his face a certain way or moved his shoulders. He seemed to purr along, emitting an almost audible buzz, like a string of high tension wire advancing across a meadow, shiny and ominous and marked for danger. It was at that moment I realized as much as I was attracted to the man, I feared him, too.

The waiter came back with a bottle of wine. How had I missed Ted's order? Had I been so engrossed in him I had shut out everything around me. In my business, that kind of selective attention can be deadly.

Ted tasted the wine and nodded to the waiter. My glass was filled and we toasted, our eyes meeting and holding. I sipped, surprised by the delicate dryness of the chablis. He leaned back and sighed, eyeing me through half-lidded eyes. "Tell me what you've found out."

How I dreaded those words from him. I had decided to give him the usual thingsare-progressing-as-well-as-can-be-expected speech, but his look persuaded me to be truthful. "I just returned from Vero Beach. I went there to talk to Jerry Ramirez."

He sipped his wine carefully before saying, "Who's he?"

"A friend of Roberto Ramon. Apparently Roberto died in Jerry's living room in Tallahassee."

Ted studied his wine glass. "What did he tell you?"

"Only what I already knew."

Ted's hand reached over and touched mine. His hand moved so slowly and then settled on mine so softly, it made me aware of the contrast in Ted's styles and mine. I am an impulsive person who runs either hot or cold about things. I get wired up and fly off to see a suspect or tail somebody, then come home or go back to my office and flop down, exhausted for hours.

Ted gave me the impression he never moved quickly and certainly didn't get tired. Everything he did had a measured, yet relaxed quality to it. At the same time, he was full of energy, as if he was driven by some inner time clock that ran very slowly, but inexorably toward a goal. He took his time, checked out the territory, then acted. The only exception to that had been his visit to Lieutenant Jefferson's office, and I was beginning to think that had been a ploy of some kind.

Although I was self-conscious as a school girl before her first piano recital with Ted, I was also able to slow down and adjust my usual frenetic pace to half-time. At first it felt strange and I was impatient to charge ahead. After my second glass of wine, I sighed and relaxed back into the cushion behind me.

"Like the wine?" he said.

"Yes."

"Good. Shall we order?"

The meal consisted of small, sensual portions, each set off by delicate whirls of fresh fruits and exotic vegetables: paté smooth, with a touch of spice; salad crisp and tasty with plenty of greens and a tangy dressing; bread tender, with flaky layers and a chewy crust; shrimp bathed in a buttery garlic sauce, then lightly seasoned with some sweet and sour herbs; fresh strawberries served with a dollop of whipped cream and small chocolate wafers.

Ted's face smiled at me through it all, holding a promise of what was to come as well as a hint of something fearful and forbidden. The combination was lethal, pulling me forward toward him while I fought to keep my primal urges under control. Each course was served with a different wine, each more impressive than the last. By the time coffee was served, I'd had a tad too much to drink and did what I usually do in such circumstances --- I ordered an anisette.

I made sure I talked to him while I slowly sipped my drink. The first thing I asked was, "How did you end up in investments?"

His face came alive in a determined, angry way. "My father taught me most of what I know. He was a shrewd businessman. Not much of a father, but a crackerjack money-maker. He used to come home from work and take out his frustrations on us. I think he got a kick out of baiting us until we fought back and then smacking us around for being insolent."

"You had a tough childhood."

"Actually, it was pretty good. Compared to my cousin. His father beat up his mother until she got tired of it and blew his head off one day while he was sleeping. She was my favorite aunt until she went to jail for the murder."

"Brutal. Did you go to college?"

"Oh yes, worked my way through swabbing out toilets. My father had the money but he thought it built character for us to earn our own way. I was a lifeguard in the summers and I saved every penny for school. I was determined to show my old man that I could do well despite him."

"Was your father pleased?"

"Not so you'd notice. He never gave out compliments, only criticism. He finally died last year. He was a miser for so many years, but lost all he'd saved in the stock market. He wasted away in a nursing home for a year before he died. Being taken care of seemed to suit him. I guess he was trying to make up for the years he lost, having to get out and work from the day he was ten."

He took a sip of his wine and his eyes turned a proud blue. "He was one of those self-made men who only went to the eighth grade, but he read a lot and taught himself what he needed to know."

"That's admirable."

Ted gave me something close to a sneer before he covered it over with a devilish smile. "But what did he get for all his penny-pinching? The day before he died he said to my mother: 'I should have more to show for my life. I don't even have enough to pay for the nursing home bills.'"

"No insurance?"

"My mother had insurance. She worked for the state university system for twenty years and had a good pension and benefits. Although he degraded her every day of their life together, she was the one in the end who had the money to pay the bills. I think that was what killed him. Knowing that he couldn't even pay his own bills."

"Sad."

"Isn't it? That's why I'm never going to get myself into a position of being dependent on anyone."

"Not even a wife?"

"You mean Brenda?"

"For starters."

"Brenda needs a keeper to take care of her. She can't even find her checkbook." He took a sip of brandy, then stared into my eyes. "You been married?"

"Once."

"How was it?"

"A flop."

"See?"

"That doesn't prove all relationships are bad. I have some older friends who have been married for fifty years. They are each other's best friend."

"The exception that proves the rule. Work is that only thing you can depend on." His tone was taunting, but somehow sexual, full of male heat and the idea that money, sex and power were all part of one fabric, something to wrap around yourself like a protective banner whenever someone or something got too close.

I laughed. In a way I believed him. But under all that toughness, there was a vulnerability I could sense and it was that part I was attracted to. After two cups of coffee, he signed for the bill and paid with cash. We went down in the elevator, so close together our bodies were nearly touching. Conversation evaporated and I concentrated on the haircut of the man in front of us. We moved through the lobby and toward his car. He opened the doors for me, but made no movement to touch my hand or arm.

I felt almost relieved that my feelings were not reciprocated. It would have broken my golden rule of not fraternizing with a client. I only regretted that it was not me who saved the day. Once inside the car, I snuggled back into my seat and let the humid ocean air rush across my face and hair.

He turned into my driveway and opened the door for me before he took my hand and pulled me into his arms. He kissed me once. Hard. I kissed him back, feeling a low-voltage current building in my center and fulminating up my chest and arms.

I tried to act casual when he released me, but my knees felt weak and my head was spinning with some giddy refrain I couldn't name.

We walked toward my door, his hand on my arm, my heart halfway up my throat. My lips were so dry, I had to lick them just so I could say, "Do you want to come in for a drink?"

We spent a few hours lingering over a bottle of wine I had hidden away for just such occasions. After a bit, I turned on the radio and found a station playing romantic ballads. We danced to a few, moving naturally together, kissing and nuzzling. I felt no awkwardness, no holding back. It was as if I had come in from the cold rain into a warm cave. Whatever wall had been built between us came tumbling down and we enjoyed each other like children playing a fascinating new game with endless variations. We giggled and laughed. At one point he even hummed in my ear, a Frank Sinatra tune, I think.

We took our time sipping the wine, both thrilled by the sensations of warmth and passion encircling us. I felt myself go warm and rosy. Our kisses ranged from warm and sweet to hot and passionate. He pulled me close and I had to fight off my impulses to make love to him right there.

Later on, we took a blanket and went out by the water and lay in each other's arms on the grass. We giggled when a neighbor flicked a back porch light on and off, probably trying to discourage us from our fun. We even sang the song he had been humming, but I can't for the life of me remember what it was. I felt comforted and safe in his embrace, as if I'd been away in a far kingdom and had come home to rest.

I fell asleep a little later and didn't wake up for hours. Then I raised myself up on an elbow and studied his face for an hour until he woke up. He kissed me goodby just before sunrise, once on the mouth and once on the nose. Then I walked him to his car and he was gone. An hour later I wasn't sure whether I'd dreamed the whole thing or not.

CHAPTER NINETEEN

When I opened my eyes, a delightful pink glow was washing over my bedroom window and a pleasurable feeling was warming me up inside. Ted Sampson's face floated in my mind like an oasis in the desert of my life.

I got up at 8:30, singing and feeling fine. I was happy. Things were going to turn out now, I could feel it. A bird was even warbling outside my bedroom window. Not even bothering to dress first, I went out to my car in my robe and dug through my disguises. I'd been putting it off long enough. I had to talk to Aaron Feinstein. He was the only one left who could provide information about who killed his wife and Roberto Ramon.

We'd only met once and that was when he had already had a couple of drinks. I was betting he wouldn't recognize me, but just in case, I needed to change my appearance enough so there would be no chance of him knowing who I was.

For a woman of nearly seventy, Evelyn still has great legs. In hot pink shorts and a bright green halter, my landlady looked great bending over the azaleas. "Had a late date?" she asked, coming over to see what I was doing.

"Paul Newman."

She shook a discouraging finger at me. "I thought it was unethical to date your clients."

"It wasn't exactly a date. We met to discuss the case."

"But it turned out to be more."

"It turned out to be more." I pulled out a red off-the-shoulder dress that did wonders for my waistline. "What about this? If you were a lawyer with a sneaky mind, would this attract you?"

Evelyn gave a wolf whistle. "Are you sure that's the kind of attraction you're aiming for?"

We giggled and dug into the boxes in my back seat. I finally settled for a blonde wig, discreet sunglasses, a shimmery black suit, lavender lace blouse and my sleekest patent heels. Evelyn chipped in with a purple hair scarf she wove around my head for extra elegance and a pair of pearl earrings she had inherited from her mother.

With that settled, I went back in the house, put on a pair of sweat pants and a tee-shirt and set off for the beach. I needed to inhale some sea air and walk on the sand for a while. I still hadn't planned strategy with Aaron Feinstein, but I knew a brisk walk would help. Unfortunately, the whole time, all I thought about was Ted Sampson.

Some snowbirds were walking the beach in their swimsuits, their skin a chalky white. I knew that by four o'clock that afternoon they'd be lobster red, but I didn't have the heart to say anything to them. When I got back home, I showered and put on my get- up.

At first the wig felt funny, but after a few minutes, I began to like the look, sort of a cross between a short Olivia Barton and an old Madonna. Of course I didn't have Olivia's features or fabulous body---although mine wasn't that bad in heels and a flattering suit. I also didn't have Madonna's blatant sexuality. Mine was more subtle, I thought, especially with only the palest of pale lipstick and CoverGirl makeup on my face. I might have overdone it with the eyeliner, but then again, I did want to make my eyes attractive. I needed a tricky notion to capture Aaron Feinstein's fancy. The only thing I could think of was to pretend I was a long lost classmate who'd come to town to visit. I called his office and put on a Savannah Georgia accent to throw off Olivia Barton. Either she was distracted by something else or I was better than I thought because she was very gracious, putting me through immediately to her boss.

His voice was gruff at first, surprised. "Opal Hills?" he said, unsure whether he should admit he had a terrible memory for past life details or simply dismiss me as a crazy. He opted for joining me in my delusion of being old school chums. "Opal," his voice warmed, "darned if I wasn't just thinking about the senior prom yesterday."

I had him then. "Oh Aaron, you always were such a gentlemen. I just know you don't exactly remember me, but I'm in town for only a day and I thought of you right away when my business allowed me some time alone."

He cleared his throat as if he was about to say something momentous. "Have you had lunch yet?"

"Why no, but I wouldn't want to be a bother---"

"Nonsense. There is a buffet at Le Jardin I've been invited to and I hate going to those things alone."

"You always were a bit of a shy boy, Aaron." It was fun making up his history as I went along.

"Find a cab and have him take you to the Don CeSar. I'll meet you there in twenty minutes."

Although I hated spending the money on a cab, it was safest. I couldn't risk Aaron Feinstein seeing me get out of my own car. He was probably beginning to question my validity already and he didn't need any more conflicting facts like a Pinellas County license plate to clutter up his mind.

When the cab dropped me at the curb, I glanced at the creations hanging in the boutique to the right of the door. I wondered if anyone actually bought clothes in expensive hotel shops. I supposed some people did, those who didn't have to balance their checkbooks to make sure they could afford their next trip to the grocery stores.

Aaron Feinstein was already waiting at the bar beside the piano in the gigantic sitting room looking out over the Gulf. A few people sat on terribly-expensive rattan couches, listening to the music or talking softly. Aaron was the only one at the bar. He hadn't changed much. Same old dark hair perfectly trimmed, round face, and smooth shaven face. He'd gained ten pounds or so and carried most of it under his chin. My mother used to say people got double chins when they worried about money. I wondered if that was the case with Aaron Feinstein.

He wore a dark business suit, the kind that can cost $75.00 or $750.00, and expensive Swiss shoes. His suit was probably more in the $750.00 range, because I was guessing the rest of his weight was tucked above his waist in the ugly little knobs called love handles. When he turned and looked at me, his brown eyes took me in from head to toe. "Opal?" he said, rising to greet me when I nodded.

He gave me a bear hug so rough he nearly knocked my blonde wig into his martini. His breath smelled of pine needles and he wore a citrus after-shave that was vaguely reminiscent. When he let go and turned, I quickly straightened my hairpiece. My investigator eye told me he'd already downed at least one drink. It wasn't a difficult guess because an empty glass already stood beside a half-empty one on the bar where he'd been sitting.

"How about a drink before lunch," he said. "I can't bear facing those sharks without a little fortification." He indicated a stool next to him and slumped onto his. "This is the kind of place Laura loved," he said, looking around at the piano and expensive decor. When he scowled, I decided to see if he would tell me what I needed to know then.

I put on my dumbest southern belle voice and said, "Who's Laura?"

"My wife."

I tried to sound crushed. "Where is she today?"

He batted a hand at me, then laughed. "Laura? She's dead. Been dead for years. Places like this only remind me of her."

"I'm sorry."

"It's okay, I don't mind coming to these things as long as somebody I know is with me."

I smiled demurely and said, "I meant I was sorry about your wife."

He grunted. "No condolences needed. Our marriage was over for all intents and purposes long before she died."

"Sorry to hear that, too."

Feinstein's well-manicured hand picked up his glass and drained the remains. Then he signalled the bartender before he turned to look at me. "What will you have?"

"A virgin Mary. I have to see family later and I can't chance them smelling liquor on my breath. Uncle Charlie is a religious fanatic." I glanced at Aaron to see if I'd gone too far, but apparently the gin had sufficiently sotted his brain that he wasn't paying much attention to my chatter. I hoped he was still in touch enough to talk about his wife.

Men who drink too much usually get around to talking about their wives or widows soon enough. I tried to hasten the process. "Tell me about Laura," I said, opening my eyes into a wide-eyed stare. "I'm sorry I never had the chance to meet her."

He raised his eyebrows and picked up the martini glass the waiter had just deposited in front of him. "She was interested in anything in pants. She was also fascinated by herself and how many dresses, furs and cars she could acquire."

"That must have been tough for you."

"Not really. I had a little fun myself."

I winked at him. "Two can play the game."

He nodded and took another swig.

Sensing the time was right, I asked, "How did she die?"

His eyes narrowed and he folded his head into his neck like a threatened bird. There was a throb in his voice when he said, "Murder."

"No kidding. How awful. Those kinds of things get in the newspapers and all---" The liquor appeared to be loosening his tongue and he swung into high gear, talking over my talk, filling me in on past events.

"What was awful was they suspected me at first."

I put a hand on Aaron's, hoping I was conveying just the right amount of sympathy. "You poor man."

"The police realized very quickly they had the wrong person and someone else was sent to jail for her murder."

"Who?"

"A guy I did business with. Who would have thought he'd be sleeping with my wife." His voice took on a dark and angry tone. "He got what was coming to him."

"Is he still in jail?"

"Rumor has it he's out and is trying to prove someone else murdered Laura. What a schmuck." He took a big gulp of his drink, set it down and took hold of my hand.

"Enough of me. What have you been up to since school?"

I giggled, girlishly. "But I want to hear more about your wife and how she was murdered."

He slumped back from the bar. "What is this, twenty questions? I'm not talking anymore about her. She's dead." His anger quelled and he looked at me with dilated pupils. "What about you? I want to hear all about what you've been up to."

I pushed back a clump of blonde wig and said, "I never speak of scandal on an empty stomach. What about that lunch you spoke about? I promise to tell all after lunch."

He laughed softly, then stood up and signed the check. Although he'd downed at least three martinis, he showed no outward effect. Either the guy was a sponge inside or he was very good at metabolizing alcohol. His face had turned slightly more pink and his breath was definitely something to stay away from, but he walked a straight line and only showed he might be feeling the results of his romance with gin when he missed the entrance to LeJardin and almost walked into a banquet room instead.

I tapped his arm and gently pulled him into the room with buffet tables. He took out a crumpled invitation and handed it to the black-suited man at the door. Evidently it was the right place because the man smiled, nodded and showed us to a table.

I gazed at the buffet, realizing how hungry I was. There was quite a spread of food, all beautifully placed on shining linens. We helped ourselves to shrimp, broiled chicken and a salad of greens, then made our way back toward our table.

A tall red-haired man who blinked nearly non-stop came up and started talking about the real estate business to Aaron. They almost got into a fight over who owned a new condominium being built in Treasure Island, but a short woman with unruly gray hair came up and intervened by dragging the tall red-haired man away.

Aaron ordered a bottle of wine and then turned to me. "See? This place is a zoo. People like to pick fights with me lately."

"He seemed a very rude man. Don't let it bother you."

He smiled, a kind of rakish smile, and said, "I won't let it bother me if you won't let it bother you."

After a few swigs of wine, his hand found my thigh. I tried not to tense up, but I couldn't help groaning in anguish when his fingers began to move up my leg. Luckily he took it for a moan of passion and smiled at me through half-lidded eyes. I patted his hand and then gave it a fond squeeze. "Let's not start anything here we can't finish," I murmured in what I hoped was a sexy voice.

The truth was he scared me more than a little and my stun gun and tear gas were sitting in my car under my seat. Not that I could have used it in those close surroundings, but they might have given me the feeling of confidence I was fast losing.

He babbled to me about some old school friends and I made noncommittal answers which seemed to please him. We both picked at our food and he finished most of the bottle of wine. A couple of men in business suits came by for a few minutes and talked business deals with him, but he brushed them off. He wanted something only a woman could provide and I was the unwilling volunteer.

He still didn't seem drunk, but his face had taken on a devastated look. Whatever was wrong with him went deeper than the liquor he was consuming at a record rate. He seemed to be grasping for life from the edge of a whirlpool of drink. His facial expression erased my fear and tugged at my sympathy like the gentle night breeze off the Gulf that invites you in for a dip.

I knew he was an accident looking for someplace to happen and I almost got up from my chair and left him in the restaurant. Instead, I raised my wine glass and toasted him: "To better days."

He nodded and clanked his glass against mine before he drank. His eyes were getting that glazed, bloodshot look of too much alcohol and a pink sheen had taken over his cheeks and forehead. "To hell with the past!" he almost shouted and a patron or two looked over at us.

I patted him on the back and crooned to him softly, hoping to quiet him enough to get him talking again.

He set his glass down and stared into it. "The past isn't so easy to forget. I tried to wish it away, but people don't get what they want in this life. I suppose I sound like a self-pitying wimp to you." Aaron Feinstein swallowed hard, sniffed and straightened up in his chair. "You don't want to hear this bull. What about you? Does your past stink, too?"

I shrugged. "I've had my share of bad luck and bad relationships."

Something glinted in his eyes. "I knew it. I had a feeling you had some bad times. People say I'm a little psychic."

That was the first time I'd heard that about Aaron Feinstein, but then most people have little idea how others perceive them or vice versa.

He went on talking to his glass as if I was only a piece of furniture in one of his rooms of the past. "Even when I was a kid in school, I could tell when the teacher was going to call on me or when a girl had the hots for me. Course I was better looking then." He gazed down at his belly.

"You're not so bad looking now," I said. I wanted him to feel better so he'd talk about his wife again, but not so good that he wanted to slip under the sheets with me.

He smiled and sputtered through his lips. "Go on. I'm out of shape for sure." He gazed around the room. "See that guy over there. Sid Sheldenberg. He runs in marathons or something. And Rudy Tempers is shacked up with eighteen-year-old twins. Next to them I'm a has-been."

I could see where he was going and I didn't like the direction. "It's hard to keep firm after thirty. I try to walk on the beach everyday."

"Good for you," he said, obviously not ready for any kind of advice. He waved a hand at the waiter. "What about a brandy?" he asked me.

"None for me," I said.

"But you don't have to drive. I'll have my limo drop you at your hotel."

"That's not the point. I'm a little dizzy already."

Aaron Feinstein grinned. "I never used to be able to hold my liquor either. Then I discovered a little trick. I have a glass of milk before I take a drink. Coats the stomach. An old drunk taught me that one."

I didn't believe his trick worked. Especially since dark circles had taken up residence under his eyes and his face had begun to sag toward his chin as if it was thinking about sliding off.

He cocked an eyebrow at me. "You married, Opal?"

"Nope. I was, but it didn't work out."

"Most marriages don't. We end up just tolerating each other. What do you do for a living?"

That was the one question I dreaded. I had decided to tell him I was a writer, but he interrupted my thought.

"Wait, don't tell me. I like to guess these things. Part of the psychic thing." His gaze slipped from my eyes to my breasts as if he'd like to lay his head there and take a rest. His hand came out and took mine. He looked at the palm. "These are not the hands of a working woman. You must be independently wealthy."

I giggled. "Nope. Guess again."

"You're pretty enough to be a model."

"Not quite."

His gaze went over me once more. I squirmed under the pressure and I could feel the perspiration building under my arms. He said in a husky whisper, "You're not a policewoman, are you?"

I laughed shakily. "You have one more guess."

"Why do I think you're a cop?"

"No questions, only guesses."

"I give up. Give me a hint."

"It's nothing I can talk about."

He leaned closer. "You're not with the CIA, are you? Jeff Hogsteter joined right out of school." He looked at me with surprise." You don't seem the type."

"There is no type."

Aaron Feinstein nodded. "Guess you're right about that." The thought I might be spying on someone seemed to intrigue him. He came fully alive, his face taking on an expression of interest. "You're not looking into some drug case, are you?" He circled his lips with the tip of his thick tongue.

"We won't talk about it here. It's classified."

He nodded again. "We could talk upstairs. I have a suite I lease for the company sometimes. I can get some more wine, or coffee, if you prefer."

I picked up my bag. I didn't want to get into a compromising position, but he had enough booze in him to slow him down. When he stood up, he swayed to the right and I knew he wouldn't be bedding anyone in the next few hours, at least not me.

We went up in the elevator. I watched his face in the mirror. The flush on it had faded and now he looked pale, nearly a sickly gray color.

We walked along the soft carpet toward a room near the end of the hall. He fumbled in his pocket for a key, then groped at the lock. The curtains were drawn closed so even though it was late afternoon, it was dark inside. He stopped in front of me and let me walk into him. His body fell against mine. It felt like one of those extra firm pillows.

His mind had turned unfriendly: "Have you ever killed anyone?"

"No. Have you?"

He pulled me closer. "This isn't a joke."

"I didn't think it was." He was offering me something, but I wasn't sure what it was.

"You're an exciting woman, Opal," he said, sounding more depressed than excited. Mr. Feinstein was a crude operator, moving too fast for a man of his supposed experience. I chalked it up to the liquor he'd consumed. But somewhere in the back of my mind I wondered if he was emotionally disturbed. Everything he said played off me with a double meaning, snarling and shrieking in my ears.

"You like me, don't you, Opal?"

"I don't really know you."

He sang softly in my ear, something about the way I changed his life. He gripped my back and forced his tongue between my lips. It wove around my mouth like a hot snake. I broke his chiropractic grasp: "You promised me some wine."

"Don't you want to play?" Coming from him, the question sounded strange. He leaned into me again, this time like a man about to pass out. "I know I'm not the world's greatest lover, but some women find me attractive."

"You are, but let's have that drink first."

He reached for the light switch, holding me against him in case I had plans to move. He hummed more of the song. His voice was dreary and off-key. A faint feeling of sadness floated through me that he had reduced himself to nooners with women he'd never see again.

The light stung in my eyes and the room jumped to life, bright with color and taste. It had that closed up smell as if it hadn't been used for a long time. He walked to a cabinet and took out a bottle of scotch and two glasses. He gave me a cockeyed wink. "No wine, but this ought to do."

He handed me a double and swigged his down in one gulp. Then he took off his jacket, threw it in a heap on the floor and sprawled on the bed, kicking off his shoes in the process. He hugged the bottle to his chest as if it were his security blanket. He patted the space beside him. "Lie down beside me, Opal. Talk to me about yourself."

I sat down, keeping well toward the edge. "I'd rather hear about you, Aaron. Do you live alone now?"

Feinstein stared at the ceiling. "Sometimes. Most of the time. Always. Take your pick. What about you?"

"I live alone. My family is in California."

"Too bad. My family is dead, or may as well be." He pulled out his wallet and showed me a picture of a young girl. "This is my daughter, Alexandria. She's hooked on drugs."

I took the wallet and gazed at the picture. A blonde woman with a look of guilt and fear on her face stared back at me. "She's pretty," I said, and she was in a lost, disturbed way. She had the fragile blonde looks of a woman who had been emotionally or physically abused and was working hard to gain everyone's approval. I handed him back his wallet and he clutched it to his chest.

"She's pretty, but dumb." He delivered his words in a monotone, but there was a vibration of dread in his voice. His face had taken on a greenish tint. Behind the tough, business exterior, I could sense his vulnerability. His breath came at me harshly through the odor of whiskey and gin. I felt a sting of sympathy for the man. He was the symbol of the people I work with, the kind that engendered both pity and fear, keeping me interested enough to stir among their battered souls.

He jerked his head to the left. "Turn the light off, would you? I can't stand it."

I got up and switched off the overhead light. I left the one in the bathroom on. When I came back, he had the bottle upended against his mouth. His throat glistened in the dull light as the whiskey went down. "Drink up," he said in a derogatory voice. "I hate drinking alone."

"I can't take any more. If I mix drinks---"

"It doesn't matter. Just talk to me. Talk to me until I pass out. It isn't as easy to pass out as you think. Sometimes it takes me days. Tell me about your work. Is it dangerous?"

"Sometimes. Most of the time it's not."

"Wally Larsen says drugs are better than alcohol for passing out. You can control them better. What do you think?"

"I don't think you can control either one."

"What do you use?"

"For what?"

"To blank out things. To forget."

"Depends on what I'm trying to forget."

"Everything. I just need some relief from all the thinking. It gets worse at night. That's when my mind is like a time bomb, ticking, ticking, as if it's going to go off at any moment."

"What is it you're thinking about?"

Feinstein sighed. "Not yet." He looked down at his body, his eyes staying on the zipper of his pants. "Can't even get it up anymore." He turned and looked at me with a cherubic smile. "Do you believe that?"

"It happens sometimes. Most of the time it's a temporary thing."

His face took on a deathly serious look. "That's what Mel said, but I don't believe him. It's a punishment."

"For what?" The room went silent and I saw him forming words, but no sound came out.

"Too ugly," he said finally, looking at me again. "Seriously, have you ever had to kill anyone in the line of duty?"

"No."

"Did you know somebody's trying to set me up?"

"Who?"

"I have ideas, but no proof."

"Tell me your ideas."

He blew out a gust of used air. "Time isn't right yet."

He reached across my face and touched my hair. "You're sweet, Opal. Did anyone ever tell you that?"

"Not recently."

"Do you know anybody who kills people?"

"No one I can put you in touch with. Who do you want to kill?"

"A guy who they tell me is out to get me."

"No name?"

He shrugged. "I know it, but it won't mean anything to you. He's not from the old days."

"Does he live here?"

"I don't know where he lives." His eyes narrowed and the look of liquor receded on his face. "Who are you?"

"Opal. I'm Opal."

Feinstein's face pulled into lines of anger, then he laughed, a shrill, dangerous laugh. "Sure, and I'm the Pope."

We sat in silence for a moment, then a look of pain crossed his eyes and he reached for his jacket. His body was too anesthetized to make the moves. He fell back on the bed. In a weary voice he said, "What do you want with me?"

"Nothing."

"No, you want something, but I can't figure out what it is." He yawned. "Maybe it's just as well." He closed his eyes and started to snore. When I was sure he was asleep, I reached over and retrieved the wallet which had fallen out of his hand. In it I found the usual credit cards, voter registration identification, another picture of his daughter when she was five or six, his social security number, business cards from his insurance agent and a few other people, a driver's license, and an AAA emergency road service information card. He also had four twenties, a fifty and five ones. Folded neatly and tucked behind the picture of his daughter was a new hundred dollar bill. For a man's billfold, it was neat and relatively empty. No clues there.

I stood up and went over to his jacket. No black diary with gold trim, but in the inside pocket I found something better, a slip of paper with important information on it. My heart did a little flipflop when I unfolded it. Ted Sampson's name and phone number jumped up at me like a pack of angry fleas hungry for blood.

CHAPTER TWENTY

I left Aaron Feinstein sleeping and hurried out of the Don CeSar. A few doubts flickered in my mind about Feinstein. I wasn't sure he was the dangerous man Ted Sampson said he was, but I couldn't prove it one way or the other. The diary was the key to the case. If it wasn't in Feinstein's possession and Olivia hadn't seen it at work, maybe it was in his house. With him safely tucked away in an alcoholic stupor at the hotel, I couldn't think of a better time to search his house.

I pulled over and parked at a gas station. While the attendant filled up my tank, I found Aaron Feinstein's home phone number and called it. A woman with an alto voice from some midwestern state picked up on the third ring.

I poured on the Savannah accent. "Hello, this is Opal Hills. I had lunch with Mr. Feinstein and I'm supposed to meet him at his house this afternoon. Is it all right if I come over?"

The voice turned protective. "I don't know. Mr. Feinstein didn't tell me anything about any visitors."

"Poor Aaron. You know what a bad memory he has. Call his secretary, that nice Ms. Barton. She'll tell you we had a luncheon appointment. I'll just give you a ring back in a minute."

The woman agreed, possibly because she feared losing her job if she alienated a friend of her employer. After I'd paid my gas tab, I called her back and she sounded more gracious, inviting me to come by as soon as I wanted. I hate lying to people and try to avoid it, but when a case doesn't come together a hazy sense of panic starts to flow inside me, clouding my judgement and slowly erasing a layer or two of moral fiber.

It was easy to find the Feinstein house, a vaguely Spanish structure. It covered one corner of a prime residential section, but was shielded from view by a high stone fence. Luckily, someone had left the metal gate open. I drove up the narrow driveway, riverstones kicking up behind me as I went. The house was substantial: three stories of white stucco with red tile roofs. Blue awnings covered most of the windows. A copper cornice rose above the front door. It looked like a useless addition someone had thought would add class to the architecture, but the attempt failed. The Feinstein residence had none of the warmth and charm some of the other homes on the block had.

The surrounding land was equally uninteresting, except for rows of pansies near the door, in rich hues of purple and pink. A double garage with caretaker's quarters on the second floor stood next to the house. On the other side, an olympic-sized swimming pool glistened in the afternoon sun. White lawn chairs sat around the blue ceramic edging the pool, as if they were waiting for occupants. The lawn was well-tended, cut a trifle too short to produce a lush green, but neat enough for a lawyer's sensibility.

I parked in the circle drive. The house looked deserted, but I didn't want to appear like an interloper in case anyone inside was observing me. Acting like a matron collecting for a social agency, I marched toward the front door, maneuvering a set of stone steps with uneasiness. The house and grounds did not make me feel welcome. Neither did an egret perched on the roof. He eyed me for a minute, then squawked loudly, letting me know I wasn't wanted on the premises. I stared the bird down, until with perfect grace, it lifted off its perch, and flew away. Not one to take such occurrences as omens, I stood my ground and waited for a response from within the house.

It wasn't long in coming. The front door swung open at that moment and a woman in her sixties with wire-rimmed glasses and a pleasant face smiled at me. She was at least a foot taller than I, with long arms and legs. She wore a grey uniform and a white apron that showed traces of heavy starch. White shoes covered her size nine feet, the kind people who visit the podiatrist buy. She was stocky, but not fat. My mother would have called her, solid. Her hair was cut short, and was too black for her age. It frizzed around her powdered face as if it didn't know how to lie down and relax. She wore blusher on her cheeks, but in small circles that reminded me of a clown I'd seen in the circus. I suspected she was frequenting the same pharmacy my landlady was, searching for her lost youth in the form of dyes and creams guaranteed to make her look ten years younger.

Her smile faded, as if she had been expecting someone else and was disappointed to find me on her doorstep. Her triangular face took on a look of stoicism, but there was still some warmth left in her olive-colored eyes. "Yes?" she said, in a voice that reminded me of the way I answer the phone when I suspect a salesperson is on the other end.

"I'm supposed to meet Mr. Feinstein here. We just spoke on the phone."

She looked me over. I guess I passed inspection because she stood back from the open door and let me enter. The rooms were large with high ceilings, but there was a gloominess inside that I hadn't expected and a stale smell of cooked cabbage.

The maid led me beyond a large living room to a small study. I tried to peer down the hall toward the dining room, but she stood between me and a better view.

Her dark eyes blazed behind her spectacles. "You can wait here," she said, before she turned and walked away, leaving me to my own devices.

When I could no longer hear her feet on the carpet, I turned and looked at the room. The furniture looked well-cared for, and a faint odor of furniture polish told me she had probably just finished working in it. Two healthy purple violets stood on a metal stand by the window. Someone had a green thumb and I bet it wasn't Feinstein. The walls were done in a neutral gray and the couches and chairs were upholstered in a green jungle print that was probably very expensive, but wasn't very inviting. I sat down on one and found it too hard for me. The room didn't look like a place of comfort or work and I doubted whether Feinstein spent much time there, but it was worth a look.

I opened the top drawer of a clunky mahogany desk in the corner. Legal pads, pens, paper clips, rubber bands, a ruler and deck of well-worn playing cards were all I found. The next drawer didn't reveal much more: a dictionary that looked as if it had never been opened and a Thesaurus, dog-eared from use. I guessed someone was a crossword puzzle freak, but I wasn't sure who. No diary. Not even a clue about where it might be.

I was about to start searching the bookshelves when I heard footsteps in the hall. The maid's smiling face confronted me. "Would you like a cup of tea while you wait? Dora has just made some frosted cakes."

I hate cake, but I wasn't going to pass up a chance to find out anything I could about Aaron Feinstein. Besides, the maid seemed lonely and that's exactly the kind of person who will tell me everything I want to know.

I followed her out to the kitchen, eyeing the oils and prints hanging on the wall. They were modern and depressing. Not my taste in art at all.

Down a long hallway, a cooking island stood in the center of the kitchen. A copper hood shone above the burners and a butcher block counter held a plate of pink frosted cakes and a teapot in a bright lemon cozy. All manner of baskets, kitchen implements and pots hung above us on circular stainless steel hooks. The rest of the kitchen gleamed with white ceramic tiles, stainless steel sinks, and three kinds of ovens. Except for the corner. There, a black refrigerator and freezer stood ominous as Darth Vader.

The maid seated me at a small counter by the window, then took a white china plate out of one of the massive cupboards. In almost ceremonial slowness, she put two tea cakes on it, then poured a stream of amber tea into a matching cup. "Lemon or cream?" she asked.

"Lemon," I said.

The solemnity with which she handed me my cup made me wonder just have much such social conventions meant to her. She surprised me when she said, "I'm Mrs. Beckwith."

I smiled at her, hoping to encourage more conversation. "How long have you been with Mr. Feinstein?"

She gave me a toothy grin. "Ten years this August." She glanced up at the cleaver hanging above us. "Yes, a long time."

I took a bite of the cake and washed it down with a big sip of tea. "I suppose you know everything about him."

Her brow furrowed. "I beg your pardon."

"I mean about his daily schedule and such."

The maid's face relaxed. "He doesn't really have a schedule per se."

"What about a diary?"

She gave me a scornful look. "You mean the kind young ladies write in about their love affairs?"

"No, the kind businessmen write down their appointments in."

"Oh, that kind of diary." She consulted the cleaver again. "No, not that I recall, but then Mr. Feinstein has always been rather closed mouth about his affairs." She sat down next to me at the counter and emitted a large sigh. "He's rather like the late Mr. Beckwith in that way." She poured herself a cup of tea and put a cake on plate for herself. I watched her cut the cake into eight equal pieces, then open a linen napkin across her lap before she popped a slice of the confection into her mouth.

She chewed it at least twenty times before she swallowed and turned to me. "Mr. Beckwith used to go to his job every morning, day in and day out. He was a very good provider, you know." She reached up and took off her glasses and laid them on the counter next to her plate. Then she took out a handkerchief and blew her nose into it. "Never once did he complain of any pain. Not once. Then poof, he was gone, leaving me alone with only Mr. Feinstein to look after. Never in my wildest dreams did I think I'd outlive the man. Me, with my arthritis and heart trouble."

She was rolling along, pouring out her pain to me and I was unsure what to do about it. I decided to just wait and listen. She had to run down sooner or later. She stopped abruptly and sipped her tea in silence for a moment. Hoping the spell hadn't been broken, I said, "Just like Mrs. Feinstein. Here one day and then, poof." Her eyes flew open in a startled gaze. She seemed disoriented by my statement, but then she collected herself and said, "Yes, just like Mrs. Feinstein."

"Were you here when she was killed?"

"Oh no, it was my day off. I felt so sorry for the poor woman. Can you imagine? Hit from behind like that?"

"Wasn't there a security system to keep intruders out?"

"Yes, but it must have been turned off. The police said there was no signal anything was wrong."

Mrs. Beckwith was the first person who made me think Mrs. Feinstein's murder might have been an inside job. Could Aaron Feinstein, who had to know all about the security system, have killed his wife after all? I chose my words carefully for effect before I asked, "Do you have any idea who might have killed Mrs. Feinstein?"

I watched her carefully for the slightest hint she might be trying to hide something. Her jaw tightened and a fire came into her eyes. "Ted Sampson. The man who went to prison. He killed poor Mrs. Feinstein." Then she gave me what my mother used to call, a dirty look. "Why would you ask about that?" Her eyes narrowed and I swear something like smoke came out of her nostrils. "You're not some kind of police person, are you?"

"No, I told you, I have an appointment with Mr. Feinstein. Aaron had just mentioned his poor wife at lunch and he seemed to still be trying to figure out her death. I thought maybe it hadn't all been settled."

Sometimes I hate myself when I have to lie about my profession. Other times, it doesn't bother me at all. This was one of the times I hated myself. Mrs. Beckwith seemed to be a nice person. After all, she'd offered me cake and tea and taken me into her kitchen.

Even though I'd opened an old wound with Mrs. Beckwith, there was one thing more I needed to establish before I left the woman alone. I put on my brightest tone and said, "You know one of the things Aaron was going to tell me was who his lawyer is. I have some financial arrangements to make while I'm in town and Aaron's just too busy to help me out. He said his lawyer had some free hours, though."

She nodded. "Mr. Handlet. He's always very accomodating with Mr. Feinstein."

"Is that a Jeffrey Handlet? I used to go to school with a Jeffrey Handlet. Maybe all three of us went to school together."

She shook her head. "Oh no, Mr. Handlet's first name is George."

I nodded. "Must be a different Handlet."

We talked for a while longer, but I didn't push her. If Mrs. Beckwith knew more about Laura Feinstein's death, she wasn't telling. I left her at the front door. As I drove away, I wondered if she was going back to polish off the rest of the cake.

CHAPTER TWENTY ONE

It was a quick trip to the car, but a longer drive out the gate of the Feinstein estate. I pulled into an empty lot down the block and jotted down some notes about my visit with the maid. I hadn't been keeping my usually well-organized writings on this case and it made me wonder if I wasn't overlooking important evidence just to prove Ted Sampson right. Then something happened that led me even farther down that path.

When I jammed my notebook into the space beside me, a flash of white caught my eye as it fell out onto the floor. I picked it up and saw it was the letter Laura Feinstein had written to Dell Channing. Refusing to admit I might be protecting my client more than was reasonable, I focused on the missive, placing it in the visor above my head. Diversionary action is a perfect foil for eliminating too much logical thought.

Although I wasn't clear on much on the case, I knew it was time to get out of my Savannah disguise and put on something more business-like. I found a blue linen suit and matching pumps in a clothesbag on the back seat. I stopped at MacDonald's and changed, removing most of the eye makeup and the wig. It felt wonderful to be bareheaded again. Amazing how much heat and itchiness a hairpiece can generate. Nobody even questioned me with a strange look when I sauntered in the hamburger place as southern swinger and marched out as St. Petersburg secretary. I guess they had french fries and Big Macs on their minds, not multiple-personality women.

The building housing the law offices of George Handlet looked like something out of English history. Several different wall surfaces converged: brick for the ground story with shingles and horizontal boards for the next floor. Bay windows inhabited the lower floor while the upper story contained the straight-topped, glazed variety. The structure ended in three A-roofs and a prominent paneled chimney.

A small sign etched into the glass of the front door proclaimed: *Law Offices, George Handlet.* It didn't impress me as the kind of address a flashy man like Aaron Feinstein would frequent, but then, if he was into shady deals, he might just want someone low key and slightly eccentric. I crammed the letter Dell Channing had given me into my jacket pocket and started toward the building.

I pushed through a giant oak door and found myself in a small foyer with beige tiled floors about the same color as coffee ice cream. The walls were vanilla, hung with watercolors in abstract pastels. Plants stood around on the floor here and there and two plump rattan couches with peach patterned cushions sat by a bay window.

George Handlet's secretary looked to be in her late sixties, with white hair bobbed around her round face, shocking pink lipstick on her lips and a look of energy and determination that reminded me of my neighbor, Evelyn. She wore a flowery dress of rayon with a sailor collar and three-quarter sleeves. Her lower arms were peppered with liver spots and gold bracelets. On her right hand she wore one of the biggest diamonds I'd ever seen. When she saw me staring at it, she warmed immediately, telling me she'd gotten it as part of an inheritance from her father, a jeweler.

She was a chatty, intelligent woman, who had traveled widely and had many stories to tell of her adventures in Alaska and Greece. Since Mr. Handlet kept me waiting for nearly an hour, I got to find out a lot about Alice Bowden. She'd been working as a realtor until a few years ago when she retired. But, feeling the need to be do "something more than travel and eat bon-bons," she returned to secretarial school to brush up her typing and stenographer skills. "I can't work the seven-day a week, fourteen hour days a realtor must anymore, but ten to four, five days a week with Mr. Handlet is perfect."

She seemed to enjoy telling me she'd been in a seniors' bicycle race and had come in third. Her husband, a retired salesman, liked to putter around the house, installing shelves and refinishing floors, leaving time for babysitting their grandchildren.

Alice raved about her bosses' warmth and good will. By then I had come to believe she was completely trustworthy, so when I was finally ushered into George Handlet's office, I was surprised to see him.

He was a small, plump man with thin, receding hair. He had almost no chin and his gray eyes were magnified behind dark-rimmed glasses. His starched collar was tightly buttoned and his tie was wound around in a knot that looked terribly uncomfortable. He kept his eyes on the documents in front of him and motioned me to a chair.

He reminded me of my anatomy teacher in college, an insensitive man who used to eat his lunch while conducting open-brain experiments on non-anesthetized dogs. I had the same nauseated, fearful feeling when I sat down in Mr. Handlet's office as I did when I had mistakenly opened the door on my anatomy teacher and found out how he ate his noon meal.

"Mrs. Bowden tells me you're interested in Mrs. Feinstein's affairs." He cocked an eyebrow and said in a saccharine voice: "A little late, isn't it?"

I have never liked black humor, especially from a man with dirty fingernails, but I forced myself to say, "Yes, I'm looking into her death."

He scratched his chin in reflection and nodded. "I heard that Sampson man was out of jail. I suppose he's put you up to this."

"Could be."

He gave me a smile of condescension. "Who else would bother? It's a closed case."

"Not to my client. You seem to think it's an amusing idea."

"Mrs. Feinstein was a client of mine for many years." His gaze was direct, piercing. Something bristled under the surface, but I couldn't tell if it was grief, rage or just plain nastiness.

"You knew her well?"

"Only as a client."

I couldn't tell if he was lying or not. He didn't look the type to sleep with anyone, but once they get in a bedroom, men sometimes change. "How did you meet the Feinsteins?" I asked.

His voice had an irritating quality, like an old phonograph record stuck in a groove. "Aaron and I went to grade school together. We weren't exactly friends, but we had a few things in common. He went to a private school and after that and we lost touch. My family couldn't afford the pricey places he went, so our paths didn't cross for many years. Then he called me one day. Out of the blue, so to speak. We hadn't seen each other for nearly thirty years and he called me, George Handlet. I was impressed with that. Old ties are the strongest, he said."

"And you believed him."

"I questioned it at first, but he was obviously sincere. He always pays his bills and he's brought me plenty of business. He's been the ideal client."

"And his wife?"

"I did very little for her."

"A pre-nuptial agreement?"

"Of course not. They were already married when Mr. Feinstein recontacted me."

"Was there a pre-nuptial agreement in her papers?"

George Handlet scratched his ear lobe. "I can't talk to you about that."

I pulled the letter out of my pocket. "Is this Laura Feinstein's handwriting?"

He took the letter from me and glanced at the signature. I doubted he had time to read what was written there, but his jaw tightened slightly just before he looked at me.

"Yes, this is her signature."

I took the letter he handed back to me. "What about Mrs. Feinstein's affairs. I hear she was sleeping around."

He colored, then blanched. "I wouldn't know about that. Besides, that has nothing to do with my work with the Feinsteins. We had---have---a purely professional relationship."

"How did the Feinsteins get along?"

"Good." He stared at a file on his desk. "As well as any married couple, I suppose." I gazed at his ring finger. No gold resided there but a barely visible line cut across the skin where one might have been. I suspect he had recently severed a marital cord. Even I wasn't bold enough to open that topic. I switched to another:

"Does the name Jerry Ramirez mean anything to you?"

"No, should it?"

"Maybe not. He had some information for me, but changed his mind."

He shrugged. "It happens all the time. People think they want to tell me something, then they call and cancel their appointments." An eerie hush filled the room and I had the distinct feeling he was threatening me although his words did not indicate it.

"Do you have any idea who might have called the police the night Mrs. Feinstein was murdered?"

George Handlet stared past me, probably at the wall or door. "No, should I?"

"You must have thought about it."

"Not much. I figured it might be Mr. Feinstein's secretary, but that was only a hunch."

I stared at the lawyer. He didn't strike me as the kind of man who went on hunches, but he obviously wasn't going to share the facts with me. He must have caught my look because he tried to cover up his knowledge: "That was a while back, you know. You speak about these things as if they've just happened."

"You strike me as a man with a very good memory. Sort of like Mr. Feinstein."

"Aaron?" He laughed, a high, mousy laugh. "Mr. Feinstein is not well-known for his memory."

"I've heard conflicting reports about that." I re-arranged my legs beneath me and said, "I guess his diary would set us straight on that."

He jerked his head back. "Diary?"

"Yes. Didn't you know he kept one?"

"No, but then I don't know everything about my clients. They keep things from me just as I'm sure yours do."

He was trying to create a bond between us and I didn't like it. I didn't like him either. He hadn't done much to improve my original opinion of him. He still reminded me of my anatomy professor. Even the glint in his eye was the same. I gazed at George Handlet steadily, "I understand Mr. Feinstein had more than a professional relationship with his secretary, Olivia Barton."

His eyes de-focused, a sure sign he was thinking and probably picturing the beautiful Ms. Barton. A moment later, he sniffed, then looked directly at me. "Ms. Barton and Mr. Feinstein are none of my business."

"Did you know Ms. Barton was once arrested in a murder case?"

"No, and if she was, she must have been cleared because she works for Mr. Feinstein."

"Maybe he hired her because he knew she was a felon or maybe because his knowledge of her past would be a way to keep her in control."

"You have a very active mind, Ms. Franco."

"Thank you. I try to consider every possibility. It's the only way I can get at the truth."

"I didn't know people in your line of work were that interested in truth."

I ignored the hostility in his voice. Such reactions come with the territory. I get a lot of it and I've had to de-sensitize myself. Otherwise, I'd just crumble, fight back or do something stupid to interfere with the tasks I must do to help my clients. I smiled at him with what I hoped was gracious forgiveness and asked, "What if Laura came between Mr. Feinstein and his love for Ms. Barton?"

He sniffed again. "I doubt Mrs. Feinstein would ever allow that to happen. She was very good at protecting her interests."

"Did you know Mrs. Feinstein once slapped Ms. Barton and told her to get out of her house?"

He laughed with glee. "I don't doubt it. I told you she was good at protecting her interests."

"How about with you? Did she try to lord it over you?"

"Not at all. Ms. Franco, are you trying to suggest I might have had a motive for killing her?"

"Nope, just trying to gather the facts."

"Then let's keep the discussion on a reasonable basis, shall we?"

My dislike of Mr. Handlet was growing moment by moment. I cleared my throat and tried to clear my mind of all distaste for the man. "I shall endeavor to do that, Mr. Handlet." I took a deep breath and said, "Do you know Barry McCloud?"

"Is he in plastics?"

"No, investment banking."

"Oh, him. Yes, his name has been mentioned in my presence, however, I have never met the man."

"Laura Feinstein not only knew the man, but had an affair with him."

"As I told you, that is no concern of mine."

"What if he got mad when she jilted him and decided to kill her?"

"I doubt that very much, Ms. Franco. Executives rarely kill people."

"Some do. Besides, he has the bucks to hire someone to do it."

He consulted his watch. "Are you on some kind of fishing expedition, Ms. Franco. I believe I have an appointment very soon."

"I hate fishing. Besides, your secretary told me you were free until four o'clock."

"I shall have to speak to Ms. Bowden about sharing my appointment schedule with anyone outside the firm."

I smiled to myself, thinking Ms. Bowden had enough spunk to disobey his orders every day of the week and still keep her job through her industry, brains and inventiveness. He shook his head. "Ms. Franco, what are we trying to do here, conduct a psychoanalysis or provide facts about Mrs. Feinstein's murderer?"

"The two may be connected. Do you have any evidence she killed herself?"

"None. Mrs. Feinstein was definitely in full control of all her capacities when she died."

"I heard she was from a dysfunctional family and might have been abused."

He raised his eyebrows and gave me another of his phoney smiles. "She looked pretty good to me."

"People from abused families can sometimes look pretty good on the outside." I'd heard that from my psychiatric nurse friend, Sarah. She's always sounding off about co-dependency and how one gets that way. I felt pretty solid on my facts on that subject. He nodded, probably not wanting to get into it any further. I tried my trump card.

"Did you read Laura Feinstein's screenplay?"

He did a double take, then sank back into his chair, trying to look calm. "I didn't know she had that talent."

"Then you never read it?"

"Of course not. As I said before, my clients have many secrets."

"Do you know Mr. Feinstein's biggest secret?"

He leaned forward, his forehead wrinkling with confusion. "I told you, my clients frequently keep secrets. But that's of no concern to me. They probably don't even consider them secrets, more like errors of omission or private information not necessary for their lawyer to know."

"Did you know Mr. Feinstein is verging on alcoholism?"

I had hardly finished the last word of my sentence when Mr. Handlet rose and ushered me toward the door with his final words: "I have no more time for questions, Ms. Franco. Good luck with your case, but I believe it has all been settled, very long ago, in a trial that sentenced the real murderer."

Without another word, I found myself on the other side of his closed office door. I left Mr. Handlet's office wondering what was really going on inside his head and how many secrets he'd kept from me.

CHAPTER TWENTY TWO

The call from Olivia Barton came in about ten o'clock that night. My father's voice flew into my mind, making me remember his story about Boots Allen and wonder if it might be repeating itself. Was Olivia Barton the tipster my father had claimed might come forward to help me solve the case?

Her voice came at me in a tight quiver, like a violin string about to pop. "You have to help me," she said. "I have some information for you."

"Something about who murdered Laura Feinstein?

"Yes."

"What is it?"

"I don't have time to tell you what happened. He's on his way over here."

"Who's coming there? Where are you?"

"At the office. Come quick."

Before I could say another word, she hung up. The conversation struck me as reminiscent of a detective story I'd seen on television recently, but I was in no position to turn down information. I had to nail Feinstein and this looked like my best chance.

The glass and steel building housing Aaron Feinstein's offices had an eerie quality by night. The half-moon glinted off the dark angles of most of the building, while the corner tower suite blazed with a savage light. I parked in front and took the silent elevator up to the tenth floor. The glass doors of the Feinstein suite swung in with a creak, sending a tingle of electricity up my spine. Even with my stun gun at the ready, I felt defenseless.

The track lighting was on dim. Dark swirls of paint jumped out at me from the wall where the modern prints in the reception area had taken on a ghoulish look. Even the maroon sofas looked like creatures from another planet and the ficus plant loomed near the wall menacingly.

I hadn't figured out exactly how I was going to handle this. What if Aaron Feinstein was in there with Olivia? What if he'd already killed her and was ready to take me on next? In my head I rehearsed what I'd say and do, but the message never got to my knees which by then were shaking nearly uncontrollably.

The receptionist's desk was empty, as I thought it would be. My eyes travelled to the second set of glass doors and my ears strained to hear any voices coming from the interior. Detecting nothing, I tiptoed across the carpet, making my way toward Feinstein's inner office. I was fighting against the fear that had overtaken my legs and the nausea that was climbing up from my stomach.

The door burst open and spilled light, outlining the faceless silhouette of a tall woman. She came toward me bent and shaking. Her pale yellow suit jacket was missing a button and the lapel was smeared with lipstick. Mascara tracked down her cheeks in muddy lines. She had been crying hard and her face showed it. The blush had left her cheeks and her violet eyes had darkened to a deep purple.

"Ms. Franco?" she said, squinting at me.

"Yes, it's me. What is it? Has someone hurt you?"

"No, no. I'm fine. Nothing is wrong, I just have to talk to you."

I came around beside her, trying to steady her with my arm. She laid her head on my shoulder like a little girl resting on a parent. "You better sit down," I said, steering her for a couch. She removed her head from my shoulder and sat down slowly, picking at the upholstered arm when she was settled as if it were an insect needing removal.

She looked awful. The skin on her face had blanched to a dreadful white that even her mottled makeup couldn't revive. She must have lost weight in the past few days, a lot of weight. Her skin seemed to drip off her as if it were seeking another home. In all her thinness, something was weighing her down, but I couldn't tell what. For someone who gloried in food as much as she did, it must have been something important.

I sat next to her on a smooth cushion and held her hand. I wasn't sure if I did that to comfort her or me. "It's okay," I said in a soft voice.

She groaned, then said, "No, it's not. It's not ever going to be okay again."

I waited a minute before I said, "What is it you wanted to tell me?"

She shook her body like a duck coming out the water. Then she looked away and said slowly, "I should have spoken up sooner, but I didn't think it would come to this. I thought the past was over, but I guess it never is." Her lips trembled and her voice quavered when she said, "I promised him I wouldn't tell you."

"Promised who?"

She licked her lips and looked up at the ceiling. "This is so hard."

"Just tell me what it is, Olivia. I can help."

For a moment her eyes snapped to life. "I know, I know." As soon as the words were out, she sighed and sank deeper into her seat. "I tried to do what was right, what I thought was right. But then things started happening that were beyond my control."

"What things?"

She sighed and the air went out of her like a used up balloon. "It's all my fault."

"Nobody's blaming you, Olivia. Just tell me so we can fix it."

"I blame myself even if no one else does. I should have told you the truth, but he warned me not to."

"Is this related to Aaron Feinstein?"

She blinked and nodded. "Yes."

"What is it?"

"I thought it was all over, but it's not. It should have been over when Ted Sampson went to prison."

I squeezed her hand. "Did Aaron kill his wife?"

A shocked look came across her face. She swallowed hard before she said, "Yes, yes."

"And you knew about it."

"Yes, I knew about it. I knew all about the whole sordid thing. I thought it was all over, but it's never going to be over, is it?"

I patted her hand and shrugged. "I don't know. Tell me what happened."

She shivered although it wasn't cold in the room. "Laura was fooling around with Ted Sampson. No one knew how deeply hurt Aaron was about it all, but Laura had a way of rubbing his nose in something when she wanted to."

"And she wanted to."

"Sure. He hurt her and she was determined to get back at him." She clamped her mouth shut and pulled her hand away from me. "I thought I was helping, but I only made it worse."

"How?"

She wound her arms around her shoulders and rocked herself. "I agreed to help Aaron, then I got scared."

"That was when you called the police?"

"Yes, but I chickened out. I've been paying for that for years."

She shivered and I could see she had lost contact with the now. She was wallowing in some ancient business that predated Laura Feinstein's death. From the look on her face I knew this wasn't the time to dredge it all up again, so I didn't.

She started to moan and rock in her seat. "Laura was a lot of things, but she didn't deserve to die. She was controlling and a liar, but she shouldn't have been murdered for that." Olivia fumbled for a handkerchief in her pocket. When she found one, she pressed it to her forehead, blotting away the perspiration that had formed.

"Were you there when Laura was killed?"

"Yes, Aaron made me go with him."

"He forced you?"

"Not with a gun or anything."

I saw from the look in her eyes that her boss didn't need a weapon to control her. He had some kind of psychological hold over her and sometimes that can be stronger than any physical force. I wanted to slap her. How could she have withheld such important information. On some deep level I knew I was way out of line with my feelings. Somehow I managed to control my voice when I said, "How come you never told me about this before?"

"Aaron told me not to."

I started to scold her for being so stupid, but I stopped myself mid-sentence. Women who are controlled by men that way feel powerless to stop. Instead, I watched her carefully, trying to blot out of my mind the words she had just uttered. It had to make some kind of sense if I could just factor out my feelings from the other thousand computations my mind was doing at that moment.

She shivered again. I could hear her teeth clacking. Finally she took a deep breath and said, "Aaron told me we were only going there to scare her."

"And you believed him."

"Sort of. I was used to the games he used to play. He played a few with me."

"Does he still?"

"Sometimes, but I'm in therapy and I'm getting stronger. I've been looking for another job. As soon as one turns up, I'm leaving. For good."

I'd seen women like Olivia. Beautiful packages who've been abused or deeply hurt in childhood. They grow up learning to depend on their good looks and sometimes don't notice other people are using them until it's too late. At that moment I felt a quiver of compassion for the woman.

I looked at her and said in the steadiest voice I could muster, "There's more. What
else?"

Olivia scrubbed across her forehead with the handkerchief as if she was trying to erase some memories etched there. "I wish I was dead," she moaned. Tears forced themselves out from under her lids and her body shook with guilt. Her fingers tapped an uncontrollable rhythm across her brow, a jig of remorse and panic. Something or someone had frightened her and she looked about to break into a million pieces.

I waited, knowing that if I said something she'd lose what little composure she had left. Finally she spoke. "He's been lying to me. Promising we'd go away. That it was only a matter of time before he had everything arranged."

I could hear the cynicism rising in my voice. "And you believed him."

She nodded, sniffing as a few more tears squirted out her eyes. "What else could I do? I was in too deep. He had me believing he'd put a down payment on a house in Bermuda. Her voice went to staccato, punctuating each word with malice. "I even believed he was planning to close up his office here."

"So what happened to make you question the arrangement?"

"I found some slips of paper, notes he'd written to himself about Ted Sampson. He used to be so careful about that kind of thing, but since he's gotten into the heavy drinking, he forgets a lot."

My compassion for Olivia was rapidly being replaced with judgment. Although I'd already figured out Aaron Feinstein was after Ted again, hearing Olivia mention his name started a sense of outrage inside me I found hard to contain. "What exactly has been going on between Ted and your boss?"

"Aaron has been obsessed with Ted for years. Even putting Sampson in prison wasn't enough."

I knew I was putting words in her mouth, but I didn't think she'd get them out without some help from me. "So now you think Aaron's going to get rid of Ted for good?"

"I don't know, I just know something terrible is going to happen."

I couldn't tell if she was back in the past again or really had knowlege of Aaron Feinstein's plans. "How do you know that, Olivia?"

"Because they had a fight. A really bad one."

"When was this?"

"Last night."

"Here?"

"Yes."

"What happened?"

"I was working late. Finishing up some typing. Ted stormed in here."

"What was he upset about?"

"Something silly. Aaron was pleased. Surprised that Ted would have the nerve to come over here. Before long, they were arguing."

"What about?"

"Some silly thing. I don't remember exactly. Because I knew Aaron hated him, I was watching to see what was going to happen so I missed some of the words. Ted was furious. He kept saying, 'And you didn't think I'd find out?' Aaron tried to cajole him at first. He's good at that. Even when he's angry he can pretend he wants to work things out."

I watched Olivia carefully, trying to see if she was lying to me again or telling the truth. She seemed sincere, but I couldn't tell for sure. It was still possible that she had killed Laura and only wanted me to think Aaron had. If she'd lied to me about her alibi the night of Laura's murder, she could lie to me about anything.

She looked calm then, the only clue to her upset the streak of lipstick and the button missing from her jacket. "You killed her, didn't you? Aaron didn't do it, you did!"

"No, of course not. Why would I do that?"

"Because you wanted him for yourself. You knew he still loved Laura. He played around, but deep down, you knew he still loved Laura."

"You're insane. He never loved Laura. He loves me. He'll always love me."

"You killed her."

moved down my blouse under my armpits.

Olivia shook her head back and forth. Her mouth moved, but no words came out. Her face had taken on a look of terror. Her eyes were luminous and dark and bright patches of red appeared in the paleness of her cheeks. She blinked back tears, but they overflowed down her face. I'd seen that look before on someone about to fold.

I measured my words carefully because I didn't want to overplay what happened next. "You were in a bad relationship with Aaron, but you couldn't risk losing it. You thought Laura might want him back and you couldn't have that."

"I hated her," she said, chin trembling. A tear splashed on her chest like a drop of blood. A deep breath exploded out of her along with some words. "She ruined what we had, wanted to take back the only man I've ever loved --- you have no idea what she was like. The malicious lies that would come out of her mouth."

She snatched at the handkerchief and blotted her eyes. Then she made a few deep sighs, before she looked at me. "I didn't feel badly when she died. It didn't make me feel good, but it didn't bother me either. She was a terrible woman."

"What made you think Laura wanted Aaron back?"

"I don't know. A woman can tell those things. Intuition, I guess." She folded and refolded the handkerchief. "I knew I had to do something, but I wasn't sure what to do."

"But Aaron had a plan."

She gave me a look of surprise. "Yes, that's how it happened. How did you know?"

"What about Ted? What did you think would happen to him?"

"Ted is an insensitive, vain man. He deserved what he got."

"He deserved prison, just because he wouldn't play your game?"

"That wasn't it. You don't understand me at all, do you?"

"Maybe not, but I'm trying to."

"I never thought he'd go to jail, but when they found him guilty, what was I supposed to do? I couldn't go to jail." She looked at me with fear in her eyes, "Would you go to jail?"

I shook off the disgust that was filling me up. "What else did you do for Aaron?"

"What do you mean?"

"I have no idea, I'm only searching for the truth."

She sneered at me. "The truth is easy for someone like you, isn't it? You come along and judge the rest of us."

I had a sick feeling inside that part of what she said was true, but I wouldn't let it take hold. "Come on, Olivia, you've been lying to me since we met. Were you in on the other one, too?"

"What other one?" She looked genuinely shocked. I wasn't sure if she was the best actress I'd ever seen, or really didn't know what I meant.

I snapped out his name: "Roberto Ramon, that's who."

She shook her head and slumped down in her chair. "I don't know what you mean. I don't know anyone by that name."

"Sure you do, the Feinstein's gardener. He must have seen you the night you two killed Laura."

She blinked at me. "No one saw us. At least I don't think they did."

"You're lying again, aren't you?"

She shook her head. "No. No, I'm telling the truth."

"Sure you are."

I stood up and started for the door. I heard her behind me. She grabbed my arm and dug in her fingernails. "What are you going to do?"

"I'm telling my client, that's what. And then, I'm giving Lt. Jefferson a call." The last words I heard her say as I stormed out the door were: "Ms. Franco, wait!" But I didn't turn around and I didn't wait. I moved toward the elevator, leaving Olivia behind.

CHAPTER TWENTY THREE

I pulled over to a phone booth on Central and dialed Ted's number. The phone rang ten times before I conceded he wasn't home. I finally hung up and crawled back into my car. The suspense was too much for me to take sitting alone at home so I headed north toward garbageland and the home of Joe Latimore. If I couldn't share my find with Sampson, at least I might be able to catch Joe in a lie.

The smell of burning refuse was already in the air when I took the exit off the 275 and headed toward the trailer park. Something caught my eye when I pulled up at a stop sign. It was Joe Latimore's getaway car, the dilapidated maroon station wagon. There couldn't be two of them with fake wood panels and IRA stickers.

I swerved into the parking lot, pulled out my camera and headed for the door. If I could catch Joe Latimore without his cane, I'd wrap up both cases the same night. Congratulating myself for my stunning detection skills, I strode into the tiny bar like a big game hunter.

It was one of those dreary little places where the glasses stand on a shelf above the bar and you have the distinct feeling they're not clean. The bartender seemed more interested in watching the football game on the television set above his head than on serving drinks. A sad-faced waitress in a black uniform and earth shoes clumped around the floor taking orders, but I could tell her heart wasn't in it. The place smelled of stale beer, cigarettes and not enough disinfectant. Near the door, a couple of video games made computer noises. Three unshaven young men in jeans with cigarettes hanging out of their mouths played pool next to a row of high-backed booths. Music with a distinct western flavor kicked in from a jukebox near the tiny dance floor.

Just as there was no mistaking the maroon station wagon, there was no mistaking Jerry Latimore. He'd swapped his faded plaid shorts for a pair of faded jeans, but he was still wearing the baby blue short-sleeved polyester shirt. His paunch looked as if it had grown a few inches in diameter, and I wondered if Jerry had been snacking on the beef jerky and potato chips hanging near the bar.

My target had shaved, but his pewter-colored hair still hung around his face in greasy clumps. His lips looked less bloodless, probably because he was smiling and dancing across the floor with a woman. She was in her sixties, wearing a flowered mini-dress, inch-thick makeup and cowboy boots. Joe, you really can pick them. The woman snuggled against his chest and twirled his hair with her fingers.

"Mr. Latimore," I called from behind a table nearby.

He whirled, squinted at me, then waved as if we were old friends. The flash from the camera shot out around him in spirals of sparkling light. It took him a minute to realize I'd taken his picture. When his brain connected, he tried to cover his face. Then he got angry. "Who the hell do you think you are?" he shouted, but I ducked out the door before he could see again. A minute later he came charging out of the bar after me, shaking his fist and using more swear words than I've heard in a long time. By that time, I was half way down the block, my eyes watching his image fade in my rear view mirror.

I dropped the film off at one of those twenty-four hour places, making sure I dated and identified it properly. Those were the times I wish I had a movie camera, but they're just too expensive. Besides, I'd bet my eye teeth the waitress would corroborate my testimony. She looked like a woman who was looking for excitement, but was too frightened to go out and find some of her own.

Even without her help, the still photos might just persuade my ex-husband to pursue the case. Mike is a nerd, but he's not stupid. With his backing, I could borrow his video equipment and pick up some footage that would stand up in court. If Jerry Latimore was out dancing that night, chances were he was walking around in a few other places without a cane.

A quick visit to my ex-husband's condo confirmed my worst thoughts about him. He was stupid. I could hear the resentment in his voice that I'd dragged him away from Wednesday night wrestling. He didn't even want to invite me in. Maybe he had a female friend in there and they were practicing holds. Whatever, he didn't want me inside his digs and he didn't want to talk to me very much either.

"No can do," he said, pulling the front door shut halfway shut so I couldn't see inside. "I think you're whistling in the dark on this one. I told you we were settling."

"But don't you even want to see the evidence?"

He shook his head at me. "It would cost us ten times what the settlement would to go to court. You know how expensive that whole scene is."

"I know, but you asked me to do this---"

"Procedure. Once I found out the low-down on this guy, I knew settlement was the only way to go. Now stay away from the guy or you'll set him off and he'll hire his own lawyer and sue the pants off me. You should have never taken that picture in public. What were you thinking of?"

I felt like a little girl who had been duly chastised, only underneath was the anger I had experienced when I was ten years old and a wasp bit me on the ankle four times. My voice came out in a spurt of venom. "How stupid can you be? He'll probably pull the same thing next year when he runs out of money."

Mike shrugged and tried to pull the door closed on the foot I had so judiciously placed there just in case the idea occurred to him. I poked him a good one on the arm. That gave me just enough of a surge of courage to continue. "I don't know why I start these cases," I said, picturing myself punching him in the face.

He pulled his head back a few inches, probably picking up my rage at him. Just to taunt me a little more, he said, "Don't forget to let me see the pictures. It would be worth it just to see that woman in the cowboy boots."

"Forget it," I said, pretending I was stepping on his foot by mistake just before I withdrew my foot and jogged off to my car.

When I got back home I tried Ted again. Still no answer. I picked up Laura Feinstein's screenplay one more time and waded through it. This time something on page twenty-two struck me. Somebody named Tom Gardener was in that scene and he was more than a little cozy with the heroine. Suppose Laura was writing about her affair with Roberto Ramon, the gardener, and suppose Aaron found out? Could he have killed them both to assuage his anger?

I had no way of proving my suspicions, but Lt. Steve Jefferson might be interested in my theory. It was all I had and I owed him something.

He was on the job, as he often is, talking on the phone, bushy eyebrows moving in unison with his mouth. One of his huge hands waved me into a chair opposite him while he continued his conversation. His eyes settled on me, giving me a sure message that I had done him wrong by not keeping him informed.

When he saw I was being held in tow by his particular form of guilt induction, he smiled and brushed a hand through the gray of his crewcut. Even his eyes settled down one level from piercing to penetrating. As he talked, I stared at him, wondering what he had been like as a younger man. Sure, the forehead was creased and the nose crooked from taking some kind of punishment, but under that was a freshness and an energy that even his ornery posturing could not hide.

He's a competent man, a bit too emotionless for me, maybe a tad too calculating too, but he knows what he's doing and he doesn't try to trick me like Mike does. For that I'm grateful. The Lieutenant slammed the phone down a minute later and focused his full attention on me.

I dropped the screenplay on his desk. He leaned over, glanced at it, then looked back at me. "What's this, a peace offering?"

"No. Evidence."

"What the hell is it?"

"Laura Feinstein's screenplay. I think it contains a clue about the link between who killed her and who killed Roberto Ramon."

"Oh?" He fingered the pages, then cocked an eyebrow at me. "You're not lying about this, are you, Ms. Franco? Cause if you are, I'll get your father down here to read the riot act to you."

"You think I'm withholding information? Lieutenant Jefferson, all I know is Aaron Feinstein killed his wife and his gardener, Roberto Ramon." I was as surprised at my words as he was. I didn't really know if what I said was right, but after my meeting with Olivia Barton, I was pretty sure it was.

He stared into my eyes, then confused me by changing the subject completely.

"What were you doing in Vero Beach, Theresa?"

I gulped and tried to act nonchalent. "Working on this case. It turned out to be a wild goose chase, but I was told a friend of Roberto Ramon by the name of Jerry Ramirez would be there to give me some information."

He leaned back in his chair and scrutinized me. I couldn't tell whether he was comparing my face with all known felons or if he was considering what I had said. After a long silence, the Lieutenant slammed his fist down on the desk. "Damn it, Theresa, you've been on this business more than a week and I don't hear word one from you. Give me this story straight or I'll have your license."

"Why settle for my license? Why not just put me in jail for obstructing justice."

"Don't think I can't. Why if it weren't for your father---"

"Leave my father out of it. This is between you and me and if you want to read me my rights and then I can call my lawyer and we can sit in some dingy room and---"

He broke into a deep, guttural laugh as if I'd said the most amusing thing he'd heard all day. He slapped his thigh, then said, "Don't get carried away, Theresa, just give me the facts."

"I don't have facts. I only have suppositions. Have one of your flunkies talk to Olivia Barton and ask her who killed Laura Feinstein. Then ask her if Mrs. Feinstein was having an affair with her gardener and Mr. Feinstein caught them at it. If it all falls together, you might ask her if Aaron Feinstein killed their gardener, Roberto Ramon, too."

"You sure these aren't just pipe dreams?"

"It's the best I have to give you."

"Okay," he said, picking up Laura's screenplay, "Don't forget where I am."

"Never," I said, knowing when I was being dismissed.

"Now get out of here and get some real information."

I stood up, thought about saluting, but decided to leave before I got myself into more trouble.

I got in my car and drove over to Ted Sampson's. It wasn't that I was snoopy or anything. I needed to tell him what I'd found out and besides I wanted to see where he lived. His business card had been burning a hole in my pocket for days.

I took the Treasure Island Causeway and turned left toward the Don CeSar. When I sailed past that pink lady, I couldn't help wondering if Aaron Feinstein was still sleeping it off and how long it would be before the police were knocking on his door. If things worked out right, he'd soon be working off his D.T.s in a cell in Raiford State Prison.

The house turned out to be big and Spanish with red tile roofs and a portico next to the swimming pool. It used to be an estate, but now was divided into four apartments. A stone walk led from the street, up past some sea oats, to a wide uncovered porch. Light burned in the upper left apartment, but the others were dark.

There was no parking spot in front or on the side, so I had to pull over down the street. The porchlight gleamed invitingly, palms swayed in the late evening breeze and the moon floated over the bay as if it were expecting romance. Or maybe only I was. I crept toward the door, hoping Ted Sampson was home and fearing what might happen if he was. His name was written in pencil above 2B. I pushed the buzzer but got no response. If Ted wasn't home, where was he?

I went back to my car and decided to wait. He had to come home sometime and I wanted to be there when he did. I tilted the seat back and pulled a banana out of my bag. Usually fruit settles my stomach, but that night, it didn't. Maybe it was because something was bothering me. Something wasn't right about the case, but I couldn't figure out what it was.

I'd been hired to prove Aaron Feinstein had framed Ted Sampson and I had. But where was the feeling of climax, of the big finish? It wasn't there. There were too many loose ends.

If Olivia could be believed, she and Aaron Feinstein killed Laura Feinstein. But then why did she call me and tell me that fact? Did she want to go to prison? Ted Sampson was convinced Aaron Feinstein was still after him, but I really had no evidence that he was. The more I thought about it, the more it seemed that Feinstein was a pathetic drunk who picked up women so he could complain to them. He wasn't even looking for sex anymore, just escape from the rest of his life.

Things were just not falling into place the way they should. How could Feinstein or Olivia have followed Roberto Ramon and killed him? Perhaps Feinstein hired someone to do it, but after having spent an afternoon with him, I doubted he had the capacity to follow through on anything like that. Then again, maybe a few years ago, he did. The question that kept circling around in my mind like a greedy vulture was: Did Aaron Feinstein have such anger about his wife's affair with their gardener that he set out to eliminate both of them? The Feinstein I knew was more depressed than angry.

Then there was Olivia. Sure she probably came from a severely dysfunctional family, but would that lead to her involvement in two murders? It didn't quite add up. Something else was going on, but I couldn't figure out what it was.

Maybe I was frustrated or maybe I was just tired. For whatever reason, the next thing I did was fall asleep. My dream was vivid and frightening at first. It was night and I was in a graveyard alone. The wind whipped across my face. Somewhere far away I heard my mother's voice calling me. I made my way past crumbling gravestones and dying tree stumps to an open mausoleum. The word, Franco, was etched on the outside.

Although it was a warm night, a chill ran through me. I was both afraid and curious. Somehow I forced my feet ahead into the cold dampness of the sepulcher. Inside I heard the whisper of hundreds of wings under the sound of my mother's voice. I kept moving, although my legs were shaking.

Inside I found a black casket. It was open. Lying inside was my mother. She looked peaceful and happy. A rosy light shone around her. She opened her eyes and held out her arms to me. Tears came out of my eyes. But they weren't tears of sadness. They were tears of joy and love. She didn't say anything to me, but inside I knew she had forgiven me.

CHAPTER TWENTY FOUR

I woke up an hour later, feeling all was well with the world. Somehow my dream had lulled me into believing it was, or soon would be. I stretched, then took a sip of water from the bottle in the back seat. The light still wasn't on in Ted Sampson's apartment.

That was fine with me for the moment because I had a few more questions to ask. The case was starting to jell and only one person could provide me with the answers I needed. Aaron Feinstein was still in his suite at the Don CeSar. He had sobered up considerably but didn't exactly recognize me when I knocked on the door. He smiled at me, trying to place the face. I handed him my card and he nodded.

He opened the door and led me to a table overlooking the Gulf of Mexico. He indicated a chair next to his and poured me coffee from a huge silver pot. Then he passed me a bowl of fruit. I took an apple and waited. He sipped from his cup before saying, "I was wondering when you'd get around to me."

"You knew I was looking into your wife's murder?"

"Yes, my secretary mentioned it."

"Did you know she called me a little while ago, claiming you were after her."

He lowered his head and looked at me like an unbelieving parent questioning a child. "Olivia is in therapy. Sometimes her demons get the better of her."

"Do you have a black leather diary that you write your appointments in?"

"Diary? Absolutely not. Although Olivia is a little crazy, she is an excellent secretary. She keeps track of where I should be, and so far has never let me down."

I shined the apple on my sleeve. "Did you by any chance refer Ted Sampson to me?"

"Why would I do that?"

"I didn't think you would, but I had to ask." I played with the stem of my apple before I said, "Last question. Are you out to eliminate Ted Sampson?"

"He's a liar, but why should I want him dead?"

"Retribution?"

"I'd think he'd want that himself. After all, he claims he didn't kill Laura."

"Did he?"

"The jury said he did."

"You don't think he's innocent?"

"No. Do you?"

I left Aaron Feinstein staring out over the Gulf of Mexico, munching on grapes. What he said made a lot of sense. Ted had pulled that stupid scene at the police station to look vulnerable, needy, maybe even unstable. He'd done a good job. Lt. Jefferson had been fooled. I'd been fooled.

Had he been browsing through my resume of male relationships or did he just read women like me? I had just been grandiose enough to fall for him. Come to St. Theresa, all yea who hunger after justice.

Would I ever learn? Aaron Feinstein hadn't recommended me at all, not that I thought he would. It had all been a ruse. A set-up. Only Ted Sampson hadn't been set up, I had. But for what reason?

I was beginning to feel sick to my stomach. Ted Sampson had played me for a sucker, just as he'd probably done with Laura Feinstein, Olivia, and countless others. His ex-wife had been right about him, but I hadn't been ready to listen to her. She'd been trying to help me, but I had discounted everything she said.

It had been so long since I'd cared about anyone and Ted must have known I'd be a sucker for a handsome face and a smooth talker. Men like him can read the chemistry of a woman in seconds. He'd probably sized me up the first time we met when I nearly slid into his arms in the hall outside my office. I had been begging to be taken advantage of and he'd played it for all it was worth. I could only come up with one reason why he'd taken so much time to set me up as a decoy and it made my skin crawl to think about it. I found the nearest phone booth and called Steve Jefferson. This was something I couldn't handle alone. The lieutenant was out on another case, so I left a message for him to call me as soon as possible.

Perhaps I should have talked to someone else on the force, but instead I turned to another souce of help, my father. He usually puts on his machine when he goes to bed and sure enough, I heard his gruff recorded voice on the other end, telling me to leave a message. Since I couldn't rouse him, my only alternative was to go over to his house and see him.

I drove up Gulf Boulevard and turned onto the Treasure Island Causeway. Some joker in a Cadillac had dropped a quarter on the ground in the receipt lane by the toll booth and was waiting for someone else to pick it up while a woman in a camper from Canada was stalled in the other lane. By the time these two momentous situations were resolved, I just missed the green light by the Paradise Island turnoff.

The bottle brush trees along the causeway were looking like they wanted to bloom and I sure wanted it to be spring. Ten minutes later I made a left on 66th Street and headed north toward the Tyrone Mall. Before it was built, everybody used to shop at the Central mall on 34th Street. Since the exodus, that part of Central Avenue was slowly turning into a road of topless dancers, pawn shops and consignment stores. There was hope, a new Walgreen's mall was built there, and the City Council voted to make the topless bars illegal. They hadn't figured out how to enforce it yet, but it was a start.

Traffic was very light on 66th Street, but then it was nearly 1 a.m. I hadn't been paying much attention, but when I turned onto 62nd Avenue, it started to sink in that one pair of headlights had been following me since the bridge. At the time I thought it was probably someone who lived in Kenneth City. Later on I realized who it was.

My dad's neighborhood was a special place, thick with trees, grass and horses. Driving along part of 62nd Avenue, you'd think you were in farm country, not a couple of miles from downtown St. Petersburg. The houses were widely spaced with wooded lots in between. The air whined with the call of crickets and other night-singing insects. The road was narrow with few streetlights. Usually I enjoy the darkness and solitude, but that time of the morning my heart thudded along with fear.

I reached over and took the stun gun out of the glove compartment. Some comfort. By the time I reached the turnoff for my father's place, I overshot the entrance and had to slam on the brakes, pull over to the side and make a U-turn. I caught a glimpse of my dad's house. All lights were out. I felt like screaming out the window, but I doubt he would have heard me. He's a deep sleeper.

I managed to stall out and all I could think about were the headlights of the car that had been following me. They kept coming. I turned the key off, grabbed the stun gun and reached for the flashlight behind my seat. It wasn't there. Either it had rolled out of the way or someone had taken it. I got out of the car and locked it. An old habit I observe, even when my life is in danger. There were no sidewalks, only a blanket of thick grass that had gone brown and tangled. The dew was wet as rain and my shoes were soaked through by the time I'd gone a few feet.

The car that had been following me pulled over on the other side of the road and the headlights went out. I could hear my breath rasping in my ears. Not even my usual childhood prayer calmed me. I hate being in the dark and my light clothes made me a perfect target.

I began to run in a zigzag pattern, just in case a gun was pointed at me. I heard a car door slam behind me and I stepped up my pace. I cursed myself for not having changed to sneakers, but it was too late.

One too many quick steps and I was down on the grass, a searing pain shooting up my left foot. I'd injured that knee years ago in a tennis match and now all the tendons and ligaments were letting me know they didn't appreciate my fall. I stopped using my childhood prayer and started asking for a car to come down the road --- any car, even one with a boom box.

The white picket fence to my father's house was only yards away, but it seemed like miles. The metal of the padlocked gate stood out in the pale moonlight. Even if I could crawl there in time, there was no way I could get it unlocked. I turned over on my back and got my stun gun ready.

I swore a few more times at myself for not keeping up with target practice. Over the years, I'd lulled myself into believing what I did wasn't dangerous. Now it was all coming back to haunt me like a third-rate horror movie.

My dad had left his car outside the gate that night. That in itself was not unusual. He does it when he's too tired or lazy to bring it in the garage. My heart doubled its beat. If I could only crawl behind his old Buick, at least I'd have some cover. I'd probably need it because my hands were shaking so badly I couldn't steady the gun.

I heard the squeal of brakes down the road and then a car backing up at high speed. A sudden wash of headlights blurred my vision as the vehicle pulled closer. I rolled toward to the road. "Help!" I shouted. "Call the police!"

The car spun by, spewing a cacophony of rap music at me. The driver, a boy of not more than seventeen, was staring straight ahead, his bush of long hair bouncing up and down to the music. I doubt whether he could have heard a nuclear blast, let alone my wounded cries.

The only good he did was illuminate the car on the side of the road, the one that had been following me. Please don't let it be Ted, I prayed.

Bad luck. It was Ted's BMW.

Either Olivia had called him or he had planned all along to do me in.

I rolled my body toward Dad's car, hearing footsteps charging toward me from across the road. Ted's footsteps. He had to have a gun or maybe he was carrying some blunt object to do me like he probably had Laura and Ramon. I groaned, a weak, disbelieving groan. Even though I knew he had set me up, I hadn't really figured out exactly what he'd meant to do. Now I had.

I glanced back at Ted. He was running along the grass in precise steps, like a long distance runner. He carried something in his hand, but I couldn't see what it was. My only hope was that he'd trip and break an ankle, but he'd been smarter than I and his rubber-soled shoes seemed to cling to the sod as if they were cleats. Through the mist of my pain I shouted, "Stop. I've got a gun and I'm not afraid to use it."

I think he laughed, but I'm not sure. He just kept coming, probably knowing I was wounded and scared to death. A light went on in my father's house and my lips started to pray he'd come outside soon enough to save me. "You can't get away with this, Ted," I shouted, hoping to draw some attention from the neighbors.

He dropped his pace down to a walk once he saw my body lying on the ground. His voice was just loud enough for me to hear. "Sure I can. It'll serve Aaron right."

"Aaron?" I shouted, "Is that what this is about?"

He stopped running and positioned himself on the other side of the car so I couldn't get a good shot off. "He put me in prison for a murder I didn't commit, now I'm going to do the same for him."

I groaned. "Me?"

"You. Olivia is ready to swear Aaron was afraid you'd reveal he killed his wife and Ramon."

"Why don't you just talk to the police about that. He'll go to prison for sure. There's no statute of limitations on homicide."

"He won't go to jail on that. Lawyers and rich folks can get off. If you qualify in both categories, you're sure to."

"That's not always true, what about---"

"You're my guarantee that he will go."

I was grabbing at straws, hoping against hope my dad would stick his shotgun out the window and send Ted Sampson skittering across the highway. I shouted as loud as I could: "You'd kill me just to make sure Aaron Feinstein pays."

Moonlight glinted off his eyes. "That's right. Enough talk. Time to die."

I heard the safety go off on his gun and tried to roll under the car for protection. My leg was throbbing with pain, but it was my heart that ached. My life flashed before me just before he stepped around the fender of my father's car.

A shot rang through the moist morning air. My stun gun knocked Ted Sampson to the ground and he lay there, silent. My father came on the run, his shotgun keeping the downed man at bay until I heard the roar of sirens along the road.

The police took Ted Sampson away and I swore to myself I'd never fall for a client again. We watched until their car lights disappeared, then my father put his arm around my shoulder and walked me back to the house. For the first time in a long time I let my body relax. Only then did I feel the tears tracking down my face. Although I was pretty shaky, I sensed something above me. Maybe it was my mother smiling down on us.

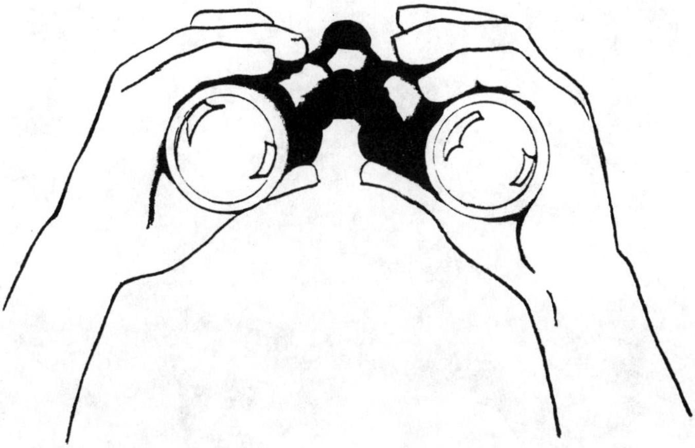